NIGHTHAWKS

And Other Stories

MICHAEL ANDERSON

ISBN: 978-0-9570452-3-1

Published by

JMHA
Publishing

DEDICATION

This is for all the people I know who encouraged me and not least those who spend their hard-earned cash to read my books. Thank you all!

CONTENTS

Giorgi and Kekela   1

Relative Values   13

A Dwelling Place for Dragons   37

A Place of Her Own   71

Soulmates   107

Best Served Cold   119

Touch Up   135

In Bad Odour   165

Vindolanda   191

Nighthawks   229

About the author   247

Giorgi and Kekela

Winds' roar and blowing clouds -
This is what their souls reflect?
They will yet take up new leaves
And their crowns return once more

Iv. Janvris q'vavilebi upliscixeši
(January flowers at uplistsikhe)

Ana k'alandadze: Four Poems

It was when Giorgi realised how much he loved Kekela that he decided to kill himself. It was Sunday and mid-morning and it was a beautiful day. The sun's warmth soaked into him and into the rough stone wall behind him. He sat outside his house on the rickety bench his father had made, its wood weathered to silver grey and worn smooth with many years of use. Kekela stood next to him, gazing at him with her liquid dark brown eyes fringed by impossibly, fascinatingly long lashes. He stroked her absently, enjoying the feel of the warm life coursing through her and the silkiness of her black hair.

He thought nostalgically of his parents. His father had been lucky, he thought. He had passed away on this very bench with his wife and child alive and well inside the house. Here one minute, gone the next. *He* hadn't had to bear the terrible burden of watching helplessly as the woman he loved faded and went away until finally all that remained was her empty husk.

Giorgi felt moisture on his cheek and wiped away a tear. Rough stubble rasped against his knuckles. He hadn't shaved for days, not that it mattered. What after all was the point? Unless he made the half hour trek into the village he hardly ever saw anybody. And his little smallholding wasn't on the way to anywhere. As if sensing the increasing darkness of his thoughts Kekela nuzzled his hand and licked it.

Her name meant beautiful, and to him she was. Her coat was almost black, with delicate brown socks on all four legs and a little circle of the same light brown around her huge, expressive eyes. Her mane and tail were long and glossy and jet black. She was affectionate and could sense his moods, and he in turn had found himself returning her love - quiet, undemanding and unconditional. But today, as he thought about Mariam and his parents and his life the way it was now, it came as a shock to Giorgi to realise the extent to which his entire emotional life was invested in Kekela.

My God, he thought. *There is not a single human being I truly care about any more. Well, maybe Konstantin and Luka. But they are just friends and would hardly miss me if I were gone. And Kekela, wonderful animal though she is, is a mule. That is what my life has come to. The only creature on the face of this planet that really cares about me is a mule.*

He got up and went into the house, the welcome coolness inside the thick stone walls like balm after the gathering heat outside. He gazed around him with the disorienting sensation of being a stranger and seeing it for the first time. Like most things in the countryside these days, it was not exactly in the best state of repair. But he loved the pale blue wash on the walls. It had the merest hint of green and always made him think of exotic oceans he had only ever seen in photographs and on television. There was a television in the little tavern in the village which he visited from time to time. Or on his increasingly rare visits to his old friend Luka. He had a television too, and seemed content to spend his life in front of it.

But this was his house and the paint was peeling and the plaster was crumbling and the number of things that needed attention was steadily multiplying. He tried to keep it clean and tidy because he knew how much Mariam would have hated it if he let himself go. He saw his reflection staring back at him in the little wall mirror. Shaggy black hair (toilet-brush, his mother had called it) now going grey on the sides over a stolid, unshaven square face with weary, haunted eyes. The mirror's mottled and stained silvering made him look as if he had some leprous disease.

He sat down heavily on the bed and ran his hand over the bedspread, heavy dark brown velvet with huge gold embossed flowers. How she had loved that piece of cloth. He lifted a fistful of the material to his nose and inhaled deeply and could almost imagine she was still there, that her warm body had lain under the cover only hours earlier. But it had been a year now. He sighed and let go of the cloth, smoothing it carefully with the flat of his hand as he heaved himself to his feet.

He went to the heavy wooden chest in the corner, lovingly carved by his father. He dug keys out of his pocket, got down on his knees and unlocked the padlock in the heavy iron hasp and opened the lid. The hinges groaned. *Like a soul in torment*, he thought. He pulled out a cloth-wrapped bundle and reverently unrolled it. It was a bottle of red wine. The discreet label announced it was *Mukuzani Special Reserve*. He had forgotten their anniversary the year before she died and had spent an awful lot of money after getting advice from Konstantin the barman to ensure that he had a magnificent present for her the following year. But there had never been another year or another anniversary celebration. Well, the bottle's time had come. How she would have loved this, he thought sadly. She always appreciated anything that was of good quality, appreciated it deeply and innocently like a child with a special present.

He had the strangest feeling that he had fallen into

some pre-determined plan and was simply carrying it out with no further necessity for thought on his part. Konstantin had explained that a wine of this quality needed to be opened and left to breathe for at least an hour before drinking it. Giorgi found the idea of wine breathing rather strange, but accepted that there were many things he did not know.

He fetched the corkscrew and placed the bottle on the dining table and extracted the cork with a satisfying *plop*. He looked down at his hands resting on the table. They were large and calloused, with coarse dark hair on the fingers. Peasant hands, he thought. It was the contrast with the cool perfection and sophistication of the bottle with its understated label that made him notice them. He had never understood what Mariam had seen in him.

He took down his hunting rifle from where it hung on the wall, checked the bolt action and took a box of cartridges out of a drawer. He wanted everything to be ready when he returned. He left the house and paused next to Kekela, patiently standing by the bench and daintily nibbling some weeds. Impulsively he put his arms around her neck and hugged her. The warm, clean animal smell of her filled his nostrils and he gave her a kiss on her forehead. He let go and walked away, conscious of the mule's eyes following him down the path.

He walked along the overgrown dirt road that meandered through his neighbour Nika Vachnadze's vineyards, a soothing sea of green that seemed to stretch as far as the eye could see. The heat of the sun on his neck, the banks overflowing with weeds with their yellow and white flowers nodding and waving in a gentle breeze, the impossibly vast blue bowl of the sky unblemished by even the smallest cloud, the desultory droning of insects … Giorgi felt as if he was in a dream and all at once he saw the first house in the village a few hundred yards away.

Where had the time gone? He had no recollection of most of his journey here, just a sense of peace tinged with sadness. He made his way to the tavern and was engulfed by cool gloom. He was relieved to see it was deserted except for Konstantin, idly and pointlessly wiping the long trestle table he grandly called the bar.

'Giorgi! *Didi khania ar minakhikhar!* Long time no see! Is everything all right? What can I get you? Perhaps a glass of *chacha*? A beer?' Giorgi shook his head and waved away the proffered glass.

'Sorry, Konstantin. I don't really want anything. It is, as you say, some time since I saw you. I just wanted you to know that over the years whenever I have come here you have always been a good listener and have never failed to raise my spirits. I just wanted to thank you for that. *Nakhvamdis.* Goodbye.'

He walked over to the astonished barman and gave him a gentle kiss on both cheeks, shook his hand and left. His friend Luka's house was only a few yards away and he knocked before opening the creaking, warped front door, its flaking paint revealing layers of previous once-bright colour incarnations like a palimpsest.

Luka was sprawled on his sagging sofa in front his television as usual, shirt open, a bottle of beer balanced precariously on his scrawny stomach. He was whippet-thin, with a long narrow face, thinning dun-coloured hair and rheumy eyes. He waved Giorgi in with an impatient shushing gesture and pointed at the screen.

'Just a minute, Giorgi, sit, sit. I'm waiting for the announcer to come on again. I swear she's got the biggest tits I've ever seen, and today she seems to have forgotten to do up her top button.' Giorgi smiled and shook his head. Luka never changed. Women's breasts held a never-ending fascination for him. He waited patiently as the camera cut back to an admittedly very impressively endowed blonde woman who favoured them with a dazzling smile and a tantalising glimpse of lacy bra as she leaned forward to wish them a good afternoon. Luka leaped up and switched off the TV.

'What did I tell, you, eh? Amazing, some the best I've ever seen! So, to what do I owe the honour of this visit? An odd time of day to come calling, isn't it?' He paused and really looked at Giorgi for the first time since he had come in and frowned.

'What's the matter? Giorgi, what's wrong?' He paused and snapped his fingers.

'It's not Kekela, is it? She's all right, isn't she? I know how you dote on that animal. A bit too much, if you ask me. It isn't natural … ' he stopped prattling and continued to watch Giorgi, who got to his feet.

'No, no, Kekela is fine, everything's fine. I just felt like a walk and thought I would say hello, nothing more. Anyway, I'll be getting along now and leave you to your eternal search for perfect breasts.' He stepped over to where Luka stood, still looking puzzled. He embraced him warmly and kissed him on both cheeks. Now Luka looked positively alarmed.

'You've been a good friend, Luka. A good kind friend. I don't know what I would have done if you hadn't given me "that animal" as you call her. *Didi,*

didi madloba. Many, many thanks.' Luka shrugged, covered with embarrassment.

'I wanted you to have some companionship, something to be there after … well, you know, after Mariam passed away. And she was born on the same day, which seemed like a sign, somehow, I don't know, I don't really understand all that stuff. I am just very happy my gift gives you pleasure. A friend could ask no more.' There was a lump in Giorgi's throat. He took a last look at his friend's open, honest face and waved without turning around again as he left.

The walk back to his house was if anything more dream-like than before. He seemed to be almost floating, as if saying goodbye to the only two people who knew him at all well had severed strings that had been holding him down, like a tethered balloon set free. His thoughts turned to Kekela. He knew Luka would take care of her, and that was the only thing that mattered. So all that was left was to savour the hopefully excellent bottle of wine that should by now be perfectly ready for drinking. And then …

He turned off the track through the opening in what was left of an ancient picket fence and walked through the garden, although it was more of a jungle now. It had been Mariam's pride and joy. He looked around for Kekela but couldn't see her, and as he drew closer to the house he saw that the door was open. He was sure he had closed it and balled his fists. Surely it couldn't be robbers of some kind. Not today of all days. He stepped silently into the house.

In the dimness he saw Kekela standing by the table and at first thought there was a pool of blood by her feet and that she had been injured. As his eyes adjusted he realised what it was. His wine! His precious wine! The bottle lay on its side and Kekela had her head twisted to one side in order to suckle at it like a baby, issuing contented little groans. He felt a helpless rage building in him. It was the last thing he had bought for Mariam and now …

'*Gacherdith!* Stop!' he shouted and leaped forward, snatching up the bottle. Amazingly there were a couple of centimetres of wine left. Kekela, startled, shuffled back in a clatter of hooves on the stone floor. She saw it was him, eyed the wine puddle on the floor and put her head down and started licking it with her long pink tongue. Giorgi stood there helplessly, at a complete loss. He felt the anger that had risen in him move up through the top of his head and depart like a puff of smoke. A smile began to form on his face and he plucked a glass from the shelf behind him.

He poured the remaining wine into the glass. Two-thirds full, he said to himself. Could have been worse. He sipped it and indeed it was the finest wine he had ever tasted. Kekela meanwhile had cleaned the floor with admirable efficiency and came towards him. He found he could not tear his gaze away from her as she deliberately brought her muzzle within inches of his face. He could smell the wine on her. The world seemed to be holding its breath and as he looked into his beloved mule's eyes he thought he saw something there that he had never seen before.

Somehow the soft brown eyes underwent a subtle transformation and he placed the wine glass back on the shelf with shaking hands as he felt his legs start to wobble as if they were made of rubber. His hands cupped Kekela's head and his entire being focused on the two eyes looking back at him. Eyes that shone with intelligence and compassion. He couldn't stop himself.

'Mariam?' he whispered. 'Mariam, can it be … ' the mule nodded its head emphatically and her prehensile lips planted a very wet kiss on his cheek.

*

It was about an hour later when Konstantin and Luka trudged up the path to the house, sweating and wearing worried frowns. They stopped in their tracks.

Giorgi was sitting on the old bench and Kekela was sitting on the grass at his feet, legs folded neatly under her body and her head cradled in his lap. He was stroking her mane and murmuring to her, smiling and laughing as if the mule had said something amusing. He saw them and waved, lifting up Kekela's head with a tenderness that moved both his visitors even if they were not quite sure why.

'Luka! Konstantin! How wonderful to see you again! Isn't this the most glorious day God ever made on this earth? Go inside! I will be with you in a minute.' They made their way into the main room and Luka's eye fell on the rifle propped against the wall and the box of shells next to it. Konstantin saw it too and they exchanged a long look as Giorgi came in behind them.

'Going hunting?' asked Luka casually. Giorgi looked puzzled and then saw the direction of their gaze.

'Oh, that!' he said, and laughed. 'Yes, I was going to shoot something but it turned out to be much too beautiful a day!' He carefully hung the rifle back on its brackets and tossed the shells into a drawer, slamming it shut.

'So, let me get you a drink! The wine's all gone but I think I have beer! There should a few bottles of *Natakhtari* in the cellar – they should be quite cool. Sit! Sit!' He seemed distracted for a moment and laughed apologetically

'Just give me a moment – I forgot something outside. Make yourselves comfortable.' He disappeared around the corner and a moment later they thought they heard him whispering and stared at each other, then shrugged. They had obviously misheard. But it sounded as though he had said *Miq'varkhar, Mariam, miq'varkhar* …

I love you, Mariam, I love you.

Relative Values

No object is so beautiful that, under certain conditions, it will not look ugly.

Oscar Wilde

Fiona turned men's heads, and she knew it. Curls cascaded to her shoulders with contrived artlessness, spun gold against her tanned, unblemished skin. Her wide blue eyes were set symmetrically in an oval face of baby-doll innocence despite full, carefully made up red lips. The sheath dresses she wore hugged her bountiful figure, and when she walked away on her stiletto heels the interplay of her well-honed buttocks beneath the clinging material made it hard to tear one's eyes away. Even for a woman, thought Alice and sighed. *Like two water-filled balloons doing a slow rumba,* she had overheard one of the managers saying to a colleague as they both stood lost in male admiration and a sort of harmless generic lust.

She was just so bloody perfect. God, what it must be like to look like that and have men drooling over you wherever you went. She felt tears of self-pity forming and hurried to the loo, locking the door and leaning against the wall with her eyes closed. Slowly, against her will, she opened them and gazed at her reflection in the mirror. She regarded herself with a dispassion borne of long practice as she made a melancholy inventory of what the outside world saw.

Her wide hazel eyes were her best feature, she had decided long ago. Sadly they were let down by almost everything else. Her eyebrows were thick and dark and mannish. She knew she could do something about that, but whenever she thought about it and the time and the pain involved she also thought, *what's the point?* Her jaw was too square, her face somehow asymmetrical, her lips too thin, her ears too big ... she closed her eyes again and angrily brushed away the tear that had determinedly succeeded in its bid to

14

escape despite her best efforts. God, she should be used to it by now. She was always angry with herself when she had a momentary lapse like this. She heaved a long, shuddering sigh and straightened up, squaring her shoulders like a fighter about to go into the ring. She flushed the toilet even though she hadn't used it, just in case anyone wondered what she was doing in there. *Fat chance,* she told herself. She caught a final glimpse of herself as she unlocked the door and made a mental note to wash her hair when she got home. It was looking flat and mousy and horrible. The way it nearly always looked to her. She bumped into Joanna as she emerged from the loo.

'Are you all right?' she asked Alice. 'You look a bit pale, that's all.' *I always look a bit pale,* the voice in her head said with its usual trace of bitterness. *Or make that pasty.* Joanna was one of the nicer ones, but even she was unthinkingly cruel without realising it sometimes.

'No, I'm fine, really!' replied Alice, putting on a bright smile. 'I'm always a bit pale!' She felt a moment's mild pleasure at the discomfort on Joanna's face, and then felt guilty. But only the tiniest bit. They went to the coffee machine in the little kitchen and found themselves squeezed in with Fiona, who was talking on her gleaming new iPhone.

'Well, darling, she'll just have to lump it won't she! I mean, *really!* Do you expect me to stay in some ghastly local pub while you swan about at the big house? Just stand up to the old dragon for once! Okay, call me when you know. Kissy kissy, you silly boy! Later!' She turned to them and rolled her blue eyes.

'You wouldn't believe it, would you. He's such a

hunk, a grown man, ex para no less, and he turns into a little boy when it comes to his mother. Or the old dragon as I call her. She never misses a chance to try and make me feel unwelcome! Me! No room this weekend indeed! You could put up his whole bloody regiment in that gloomy old pile!' She drew a deep breath and her already impressive breasts seemed to inflate even further, making Alice step back instinctively. Her gaze travelled cursorily over Joanna and lingered for a moment on Alice.

'But then you wouldn't know about this sort of thing, would you,' she said. Her smile was superior and condescending and Alice had to control an overwhelming desire to punch her and wipe that overbearing look off her perfectly made up face. It clearly occurred to Fiona to wonder why she was wasting her time with them and she swept out of the kitchen. The two of them watched her curves disappear elegantly around the corner and Joanna made a face.

'Stuck up bitch,' she muttered, but there was no real malice in her voice. Joanna was one of those people who always seemed to exist in an even plane with few extremes touching their lives. Her features, figure, clothes and personality were all in harmony, pleasant but eminently forgettable, and she hardly ever seemed to have a strong opinion about anything. Alice, however, often felt the tides of the ocean of sadness that was always within her rising and slopping over her inner defences.

It was lunchtime the following day and the office was deserted except for Alice.

'You don't mind holding the fort for an hour or so, do you?' Fiona had said as she and two of her cronies headed for the door, neither expecting nor waiting for a reply as they disappeared for another of their wine-bar lunches. Or possibly a shopping expedition in nearby Knightsbridge or the King's Road.

Alice sighed and told herself that she didn't mind, that she quite enjoyed the peace and quiet. Well, the second part at least was true. She decided to pop next door to the sandwich shop and picked up her purse. It would only take a minute and if the phone went they would ring back. She went downstairs and reached out to turn the little knob that unlocked the door.

It all happened so fast. A dishevelled figure pushed the door in hard, knocking her backwards and she fell, winded, her head banging sickeningly on the floor. Dazed, she watched the man look around wildly, spot her purse and snatch it up before turning back to the door which had swung shut and locked itself. *He smells really bad,* a detached part of her mind thought. Her lips formed the word Help! but all that came out was a croak. The man made inarticulate rage-filled sounds as he struggled with the knob before managing to turn it and wrench it open. Alice's head was still spinning and the pain at the back of her skull was getting worse.

She was vaguely aware of the sound of a scuffle and then a figure loomed over her. She tensed through the pain. *Oh God, he's come back! Don't let him hurt me!*

'Are you all right? Hello! Look at me! Are you badly hurt? Can you move?' The voice was deep and well-spoken, and by contrast to the horrible smell a moment ago she caught a whiff of expensive aftershave and opened her eyes.

His curly hair was a pleasing shade of light brown, and his blue eyes set in a ruggedly handsome face were creased in a frown of concern. Her body sagged with relief and she moved her head experimentally. It hurt like hell where it had hit the floor but otherwise she thought she might be all right. He helped her to her feet and led her to one of the armchairs that dotted the reception area.

'I managed to get your purse back – I assume it is your purse?' she nodded painfully.

'I'm afraid he got away – surprisingly fast for a down and out! But I saw you lying there and thought I had better see to you rather than giving chase. Are you sure you're all right? Is it the back of your head that's hurting? Here, let me have a look,' He stood up and bent over her. She obediently leaned forward and his fingers gently probed her scalp, making her wince when they found the point of impact.

'Poor you! You'll have a nasty bump for a while, but it could be a lot worse.' He sat down and extended his hand with an engaging grin.

'I'm Harry Lakewright,' he said, 'I don't think we've met before.'

'I'm Alice,' she said a little breathlessly, 'Alice Mayhew … ' she realised she was still holding his hand and looking into his sky-blue eyes. Some lines from a poem came into her head and she spoke them without thinking.

In time of peril, said the old man
You, who have been so kind
May speak the words that must and can
Come from the heart and you will find

That to your aid will come a gentle man

Jon looked at her with amazement.

'Gosh! You're the first person I've ever met who could quote Aldous Witherington. Let alone have heard of him! He's pretty obscure.'

The next half an hour or so passed like a happy dream. Harry was funny and solicitous and brought her a sandwich and some orange juice from the place next door and insisted she stay where she was until she really felt sure she was all right. The food and a couple of painkillers he fetched from the first aid box upstairs helped, but it was his company that buoyed her spirits and made her forget the dull throbbing at the back of her skull. They talked a lot about poetry in general and Witherington in particular – something she got the feeling he didn't get a chance to do often if at all.

The outside door opened and Fiona and her two friends came clattering in on their high heels, coming to a dead stop at the scene before them. Alice had her feet up on the leather sofa and Harry had pulled up an armchair next to her and they were both laughing about one of the poet's lesser-known humorous verses. Fiona dropped her Harrods carrier bag and put her hands on her hips.

'What the hell's going on here?' she demanded. 'Harry? What are you doing here?' Harry got slowly to his feet, frowning.

'Hello is the usual greeting,' he said softly. Even after such a short acquaintance Alice could hear an undertone of anger, and the realisation hit her that Harry was Fiona's boyfriend. It simply hadn't come up when they were talking. Fiona ploughed on, oblivious.

'I don't like you just turning up here without telling me! And what the hell's wrong with Ugly Alice?'

Alice felt as if she had been slapped and her eyes filled with tears. To be called ugly to her face, and in front of Harry, with whom she had just spent such a wonderful time … she saw him glance at her and cringed. Maybe he hadn't really noticed how ugly she was until now. He turned to Fiona.

'Really. *Ugly* Alice, is it. Well, my dear, *Alice* was mugged right here and got a nasty crack on the head, and I was keeping her company as she was all alone. I just came by because I was in the neighbourhood, but that was clearly a mistake.' Alice saw an odd sort of smile dawn on his face and he turned to her and winked.

'As a matter of fact I thought it would be rather nice for her to get away after such a horrid experience, so I've asked her down for the weekend and she's accepted – that'll be fun, won't it!'

Alice gulped. She couldn't believe what she was hearing. And from the look on her face, neither could Fiona.

'*What?* You've asked that … ' she saw the look in his eye and managed to stop the words *ghastly nobody* from coming out of her mouth.

'I thought you said there wasn't any room at the house!' she protested, changing tack. Harry smiled again.

'Well, I persuaded Mother to get Johnson to open up and clean out the three rooms on the second floor, you know, the ones she refers to grandly as the East Wing Rooms. So everything's been arranged and taken care of. Anyway, must dash, it was only supposed to be a flying visit.' He turned to Alice and handed her a card,

'Call me this evening,' he whispered, and then said aloud, 'call me in the next couple of days and I'll let you have the details.'

He turned to Fiona, kissed her formally on both cheeks and strode out, leaving a pregnant silence in his wake. Fiona hadn't changed her stance and stared at Alice, more with incomprehension than anger.

'You're not going, of course,' she said as if stating the obvious. 'I can't imagine what he was thinking. Felt sorry for you I suppose …'

At that moment the manager came through the door, his flushed face attesting to the quantity of wine that had accompanied his extended lunch. When everything had been explained to him he insisted on calling a taxi and sending Alice home. In a wave of alcohol-fuelled bonhomie he also told her to take a day or two off to recover if she wanted.

*

Alice sat in the living room with her mother in the tiny Wandsworth terraced house they shared. Helen Mayhew was in her seventies and in the last couple of years had more or less given up, sitting at home and reading or watching television and not doing much else. Alice's father had apparently died before she was born and her mother had never remarried. She leaned forward and took her mother's hand. Helen smiled, vaguely pleased by the contact.

'Mum, would you manage if I went away for a couple of days this weekend? I'd make sure you had everything you needed, and make some food you can just heat up in the oven?' Her mother looked perplexed.

'You don't go away, ever, Alice,' she said. 'Why, what's happened? Nothing bad, is it?' Alice struggled to find the right words because she was struggling with herself. It was if she had two voices arguing in her head. *What are you thinking!* said one. *Can you imagine the humiliation they will put you through? You're not one of them! Why would you want to do that to yourself?*

Alice felt herself tense with resentment, aware of the absurdity of arguing with herself but unable to help it. *And why shouldn't you?* retorted the other, angrier voice. *Your Mum's right! You never go anywhere! And it would be one in the eye for that stuck-up bitch!* She rather liked what Joanna called Fiona, and the phrase always popped into her mind when she thought of her blonde colleague.

'Where is it you want to go, dear?' asked her mother, managing to focus on the issue at hand for once.

'Well, I haven't quite decided to go yet, Mum,' she said. 'It's … ' she realised that she had no idea at all where Harry's home was. At that moment the telephone rang. *Saved by the bell,* she thought, and picked it up.

'Alice? Hello again! Harry here! How are you feeling? Good, good, I'm glad it's subsiding. Nasty bump, you were really quite lucky, could have been a lot worse … listen, do you have email at home? No? All right. Oh, I rang your manager for your number, by the way, in case you were wondering. I had a feeling you might not call … anyway, this is the plan. I assume you won't be back at work this week, your manager said he didn't expect you back until Monday

- I'll pick you up from your home on Friday – can you give me the address please – I'll be there around four thirty, it's at least two hours, maybe more depending on traffic. Okay?'

Alice gave him her address and agreed to be ready on Friday. *Well, that's that,* she thought, and her heart beat a little faster. But Harry hadn't finished.

'Oh, one other thing. You had such a nasty experience, I think you deserve a good one to compensate! A friend of mine runs a gaggle of places for women, all kinds of stuff, and I've arranged with him for you to have a day of pampering tomorrow! So there'll be a car at your door at ten in the morning and all you have to do is get into it and everything will be taken care of! Enjoy! And see you on Friday!'

Alice clicked off the phone and stood there gazing at it, feeling as if her normally uneventful life had been turned upside down. Why had she just submissively agreed to everything? She remembered how he had looked, handsome and laughing. And knew the answer.

*

At exactly ten o'clock the next morning the doorbell rang and Alice opened it to an impossibly slim and beautiful young woman dressed all in black.

'Alice? Hello! Lovely to meet you. I'm Natalie, and I'll be taking care of you today. Shall we go?' she gestured at the sleek black limousine behind her. A stocky man in a smart grey chauffeur's uniform was holding the door open, and smiled and nodded. As if in a dream Alice let herself be led to it and sank back into the soft padded leather seat. Natalie sat beside her and saw the bewildered expression on her face.

'Don't you worry, we are going to have a fabulous day! Just leave it all to me.'

*

It was late afternoon before Alice staggered back into her home, laden with bags from shops with names she only recognised from magazines. She stopped in front of the hall mirror and stared at the stranger looking back at her. Her long, lank hair had been expertly cut in a way that along with carefully shaded makeup miraculously minimised the squareness of her jaw. Her eyebrows had become two elegant curves above artfully emphasised eyes. Her lips appeared fuller and wider and she had watched her transformation with utter fascination. The woman at the spa who had worked her magic on her had been so nice, so warm and friendly. And she had taken the time to explain what she was doing and why and when she left it was with a shocking pink miniature carrier bag full of the products she had used.

And her clothes ... oh my God, the clothes. She had seen some of the price tags and reeled in shock. Surely nobody paid that kind of money for clothes? Natalie had laughed and waved her objections away.

'Otto – that's my boss – is one of Harry's best friends. They were in the army together and I think Harry saved his life or something dramatic like that and Otto would do absolutely anything for him. And in any case he has arrangements with these people – believe me, he's not paying the tag price ... and in any case so what! You're a very lucky lady – just accept and enjoy!' And Alice had. She had more or less decided that it was all a dream and she might as well go along for the ride.

She turned sideways in front of the mirror, smoothing the deep purple dress over her hips and enjoying the soft, sensuous feel of the jersey-like material. She had seen the price of this one. It had been £725. £725! Oh my God. And the other clothes ... the shoes ... the handbags ... she still couldn't believe it.

Her old, analytical self returned for a moment and she tried to imagine what a complete stranger would make of her now. Her figure wasn't *too* bad ... she would always be a bit on the dumpy side, but the shaping underwear and the uplift bra had made a real difference. And her face ... she stared hard at her reflection and saw a young woman with rather nice eyes and a strong, almost challenging jaw but overall it was not unattractive. The French had a word for it, she remembered reading somewhere. *Jolie-laide* – a woman who is attractive but not conventionally pretty. Yes, that was her now.

She dropped her collection of colourful bags and went into the living room. Her mother turned around with her usual vague smile which faded to surprise as she looked her daughter up and down.

'What have you done, Alice?' she asked. 'You look so lovely!' Alice sat down next to her on the sofa.

'You remember I said I might be going away? Well, I am, and I have been given this as a wonderful present!' Isn't it marvellous!' Her mother looked puzzled.

'Did you tell me, dear? I seem to be so forgetful these days ... where are you going? When?' Alice sighed inwardly. Her mother's attention span was getting shorter these days.

'I'm going tomorrow Mum, but I'll be back on Sunday. I was given the address by that nice young woman who looked after me today. It's in a little place called Lownton Major, out in the country.' Her mother's face, usually so placid, took on a worried frown.

'I don't think you should go,' she said, and Alice was taken aback by the quaver in her voice. *She must be frightened of being left alone,* she thought and suppressed a wave of guilt.

'Why ever not?' she said. But the older woman had lapsed into her default vagueness.

'I just don't think you should, dear,' she said firmly and returned her attention to the television. Alice shook her head. Poor Mum. Well, she would ask that nice Mrs Jones next door to pop in and see that everything was all right and keep her company.

*

It was a quarter to five and Alice was fast descending into a blue funk. What had she been thinking? He wasn't going to come. She just knew it. How had had she let herself be persuaded into this madness? Let somebody she barely knew spend all that money on her and just accepted it all and gone along with it. What was the matter with her? How Fiona and her acolytes would laugh at her. She would have to get a new job ... a car horn tooted impatiently outside the house and she looked through the window and there he was in a jaunty pink shirt and blue blazer. The car was a dark green old fashioned low-slung sports car with gleaming chrome wire wheels. She picked up her overnight bag and turned to find her mother standing right behind her.

'You mustn't go,' she said quietly. 'Alice, you mustn't go.' Alice gave her a hug and kissed her on the cheek.

'It's only two days, Mum,' she said. 'You'll be fine.' Helen shook her head and turned away. Alice took a deep breath.

'Bye bye, Mum. You have my telephone number if anything comes up. I'll see you on Sunday.' She opened the front door and minutes later Harry had stowed her case in the back seat and they drove off with a squeal of tyres.

'You look fantastic,' said Harry. 'Really, I mean it.' To her chagrin she couldn't stop herself blushing.

'You mean not like before,' she said, unable to keep a note of bitterness out of her voice. Harry laughed.

'No, you idiot, you're the same person – I think that before you just didn't pay any attention to yourself. So just relax and enjoy the drive!'

The two and a half hours seemed to Alice to pass in no time at all. Harry was amusing, regaling her with tales of his mother's outrageous rudeness and escapades from his childhood. The whole journey had a dream-like quality, as if she was somehow hovering over the car and watching this woman who was a stranger to her revel in the attention of a good-looking and intelligent young man. Eventually he turned off a country road between two crumbling stone pillars and up a hundred yards of driveway flanked by neglected rhododendrons and azaleas. They crunched over some gravel and stopped in front of an undistinguished but nonetheless imposing building. It was a substantial cube of ancient red brick relieved only by a stone portico over the front door and some weathered detailing around the windows.

'Well, here it is, Lakewright House, the ancestral hovel,' he said jovially. 'Come on, let's get you settled in.' Alice thought of Fiona's description of his mother as the old dragon and the confidence that had reasserted itself during the drive began to drain away. She also realised she had avoided asking him whether Fiona would be there and somehow couldn't bring herself to do so now. Harry heaved her case out of the car and she took a deep breath and followed him indoors.

They stepped into a cool dark stone-flagged hallway dotted with antique tables that to Alice's untrained eye looked a little worse for the wear. The eyes of dark, varnished portraits – presumably Lakewrights that had gone before - seemed to peer at her as if wondering, as she was herself, what on earth she was doing there. An old man all in black except for a frayed white shirt appeared and shuffled towards them.

'Johnson! Still holding the fort, eh! This is Miss Mayhew, who will be staying for the weekend. Alice, this is Johnson, who despite appearances actually runs this place and stops it falling apart. Isn't that right, Johnson!' The old man smiled indulgently and took her bag.

'A pleasure to meet you, Miss,' he murmured. 'If you'd be kind enough to follow me I'll show you to your room.'

Half an hour later Alice had unpacked and was sitting on an ancient four-poster bed in her room, looking around and wondering what she was supposed to do next. The house was not as grand as she had expected, although the staircase had beautifully carved banisters and there were antiques of all kinds everywhere. But the overall impression was one of genteel neglect. Some of the carpets were very worn and here and there the wallpaper was discoloured and peeling. A knock on the door brought her out of her reverie. It was Johnson.

'Mr Harry wonders if you would care to join him and the others in the library for a drink,' he said. 'Allow me to show you the way.' She followed him downstairs into a book-lined room with a high ornate plasterwork ceiling. Harry was standing in front of a huge carved stone fireplace next to a tall, imposing woman whose long grey hair was swept back over a ramrod-straight spine. She wore sensible shoes and a tweed jacket and skirt. *The old dragon.* There were half a dozen other people and they all had drinks in their hands. The conversation petered out as they all turned to look at her and she felt as if she was going to faint. *I told you so!* The voice in her head said with satisfaction. *You're in for it now.* Harry put down his drink and strode towards her, breaking the spell.

'Thank you, Johnson,' he said and took her arm, leading her towards the tall woman. 'Mother, this is Alice.' Alice put out her hand and Harry's mother gripped it firmly, not letting go while she studied the newcomer.

'You may call me Geraldine,' she said, still holding Alice's hand and showing no sign of letting go. 'All this informality would have been unthinkable when I was a gel but everything is different these days and I have learned to move with times. Let me introduce you.' She smiled and when she finally relinquished her hand Alice started to relax. Geraldine propelled her towards the group of guests and Alice smiled and shook hands and murmured how nice it was to meet them and to her horror realised she had promptly forgotten every single one of their names. Harry rescued her, led her to a seat by the French windows and brought her a glass of champagne.

'Well, you survived your first ordeal admirably!' he said, and clinked his glass with hers. Alice leaned forward.

'Where's Fiona?' she asked.

'She had some gallery opening or something to go to, so she's catching the train first thing tomorrow,' he said. They were some distance from the others and Alice thought it was now or never.

'Why have you done this,' she asked quietly. 'Inviting me here, spending all that money on that wonderful day yesterday, when you hardly know me. And you know how angry Fiona is going to be. She is your girlfriend, isn't she? Why, Harry? Truthfully, why?' He looked pensively out of the window and for a moment she thought he might be angry, but then he sighed and shook his head.

'Truthfully? I don't honestly know. Many reasons, I suppose. You looked ... so frightened by what happened at your office. And I really enjoyed talking to you – I mean that. And believe me people who know their onions about Victorian poets are pretty thin on the ground!' He paused and then continued. 'I dread these weekends Mother insists on having, and I have really been looking forward to having someone intelligent around. As to Fiona ... well, yes, I suppose she is my girlfriend.'

Alice's pleasure at his earlier words were supplanted by a flash of envy and resentment at his last statement. But she kept her face impassive as

Harry carried on.

'She is rather a looker, I know, but she can sometimes be the most dreadful snob. And the way she behaved towards you was inexcusable. And I suspect it's not the first time. And of course Mother can't stand her.' He paused and shrugged helplessly.

'I suppose I just thought it would be something different and enjoyable for you, and that it would be amusing to watch Fiona trying to cope. It sounds rather cruel now, saying it out loud. But I am genuinely glad you're here.'

A rather feeble and tinny gong sounded somewhere nearby and Harry helped her to her feet.

'Time for dinner! We're quite informal here, it's not as if this is Blenheim or anything. Come on. Cook is rather good, better than a lot of those fancy chefs in Chelsea.'

They trooped through to the dining room, sombre and wood-panelled and with a table capable of seating thirty people. Geraldine arranged them clustered together at one end and dinner passed pleasantly enough. Harry had not overstated Cook's abilities, and soup, partridge and sherry trifle were all consumed enthusiastically. After they had finished they ended up in the drawing room where Johnson served coffee and brandy for those who wanted it. Geraldine sat on a sofa and beckoned to Alice, patting the seat next to her. She leaned back, sipping a brandy and drawing deeply on a cigarette in an amber holder. Alice thought how perfect she looked, utterly relaxed and yet commanding and uncaring of what other people thought. She had yet to experience the old dragon aspect of her, and steeled herself.

'So, my dear, tell me about yourself. Harry has

been uncharacteristically reticent – have you known each other long? How did you meet?' Alice took a deep breath and launched into what had happened at the office, ending with Harry asking her down for the weekend and omitting the Day of Pampering (as she had already come to think of it). Geraldine stubbed out her cigarette in an enormous onyx ashtray, never taking her shrewd blue eyes off Alice.

'What an extraordinary story! My dear girl, what a ghastly experience for you. I always thought Harry had a bit of the knight in shining armour in him.' She paused and sat quite still until Alice started to feel uncomfortable under her gaze.

'So you have known him all of half an hour until today … I must say that's going it a bit, even these days. But you are very welcome here and I hope you enjoy your stay.' Alice relaxed back against the sofa, not realising until then how tense she had been under Geraldine's questioning gaze.

'You do realise he's been seeing that other young woman, Fiona, don't you? And that she's arriving tomorrow? I know men are often a bit … economical … about explaining that sort of thing.' Alice flushed and was furious with herself for being unable to control it.

'Yes, I do know that,' she replied, more tartly than she had intended. 'And as I understand it she is not your favourite person!' She clapped her hand over her mouth and started apologising, but to her surprise Geraldine put a finger against her lips.

'Quite right, my dear. I had no right to speak to you that way and no apologies are necessary.' She leaned back and smiled. 'I'm beginning to see what Harry sees in you,' she said, looking at her with an almost puzzled expression that Alice couldn't quite fathom. Eventually she patted Alice's knee and got up to talk to the other guests.

The rest of the evening went by pleasantly enough. She made polite conversation with a couple of people, managed to spend some time with Harry, and before she knew it people were saying good night and drifting off until only she and Harry remained.

They sat on the sofa and talked and time seemed to pass without either of them noticing it. All at once they seemed to run out of words and just sat looking at each other and then Harry leaned forward and his lips found hers. She wanted to return his kiss so very badly but something stopped her and she gently pushed him away.

'I'm sorry, Harry. Really. It's all been so lovely, like a dream. And you have been so kind … but Fiona is arriving tomorrow and what then? I like you very much. Very much. But this is all too sudden and I just can't.' He got up with her and took her arm.

'No, you're right. Please forgive me. It's just that when I look into your eyes … it's as if there is some deep connection there. Please don't be upset.' She smiled and told him she was not at all upset. They were standing next to a battered grand piano, covered with old photographs in silver frames and he saw her looking at them.

'They're mostly family. Here's me as a baby – rather a good-looking little chap, I've always thought … ' he trailed off as he saw her staring at a larger group photograph. She snatched it up and stared at it.

'Alice! What's the matter … ' she thrust the photo at him.

'Who are these people, Harry? Tell me! Tell me!'

He couldn't understand the urgency in her voice and took the frame from her trembling hand.

'Well, let's see. That's Mother, you recognise her, don't you. She really was a stunner, wasn't she? That's father – he died a few years ago – that's me with Nanny Mayhew ... ' his voice trailed off and he stared at her.

'Tell me about Nanny Mayhew,' she said, her voice shaking. Harry was still staring at her and his voice when he spoke was little more than a whisper.

'She left soon after that was taken – I remember being very upset, I was very fond of her. There was some kind of a scandal, I only found out about it from one of the servants years later. It seems she and Father ... and Mother found out ... apparently she got herself in the family way, as they so quaintly put it back then ... oh my God. No. It can't be.' Alice nodded.

'That's my mother,' she said evenly. 'Helen Mayhew. Oh, Harry. Harry. We nearly ... oh my God. You're my half-brother.' They put their arms around each other and just stood there, motionless and speechless.

*

Fiona arrived the next morning in a taxi and as she emerged Alice and Harry stood on the threshold with their arms around each other's waists. Fiona's eyes widened and she dropped her Louis Vuitton bag and stood arms akimbo.

'You bitch!' she shrieked. 'You ugly bitch, what the hell do you think you're doing? He's mine! I don't know how you managed it but I'm not going to let you scupper this just because ... ' Harry held up his hand to stem the flow.

'You know my sister Alice, don't you?' he said innocently.

A Dwelling Place For Dragons

It does not do to leave a live dragon out of your calculations, if you live near him.

J. R. R. Tolkien

Persepolis, 333 BC

Adarfiroz entered the vast palace complex and passed from the blinding glare of the sun into welcome shade between two massive statues of bulls. More bulls at the tops of columns supported the impossibly high ceiling of the immense first chamber. He had been here many times before, but the sheer size of the place never failed to fill him with awe.

Climbing the steps to the audience hall his gaze travelled along endless brightly painted friezes depicting representatives of the multitude of nations that came to this hub of the sprawling Persian Empire to pay tribute or seek favours. Scythians. Phoenicians, Ethiopians, Indians and many others bore precious gifts of spices, jewels, ivory and gold and exotic animals. When he entered the hall it was thronged with the usual crush of courtiers, ministers, ambassadors and guards. Darius III sat on his golden throne, his saturnine features creased in a frown as he plucked nervously at his carefully groomed beard.

The young man sensed an undercurrent of gloom and barely concealed panic beneath the apparent calm in the room. Darius waved him over and as Adarfiroz bowed the King whispered to a courtier standing next to him. The man clapped his hands and made shooing gestures at the assembly and they all backed away, bowing and touching their foreheads as they left the hall like water draining from a colander until only three of them remained. Adarfiroz turned his attention to the old man standing next to Darius.

He had an impressive white beard and wore flowing white robes. The only adornments were a series of obscure symbols in gold thread on his sleeves and he realised that he was one of the Magi, a Zoroastrian like most of the Persians, but an expert in divination and in reading the heavens. And, it was rumoured, much more. He looked serene but radiated an intimidating, rock-like strength.

'I was relieved to hear that you emerged from the battle unscathed, Adarfiroz,' said Darius. 'So many did not. We have urgent matters to discuss that must remain between the three of us.' He pointed to the old man.

'This is Axtya who has been advising me since the … unfortunate setback at Issus.'

Even though he remained loyal to him – what after all was the alternative? Subjugation by the Macedonian barbarian? Adarfiroz couldn't suppress his anger as his mind went back to that fateful day Alexander broke the Persian army at Issus.

He had never been one of Darius's favourites, but when the call came he had answered it with his one hundred men, men whom he had trained and armed himself. If the King had had a few thousand more like them the outcome might have been very different. But Alexander had outwitted them and when he and his famed Companions appeared out of nowhere and their cavalry smashed into the Persian left flank Darius took fright and fled, and the battle quickly turned into a rout.

It had been with a heavy heart that Adarfiroz gathered the remnants of his loyal followers and began the long march back to Persepolis. Less than half his men had survived. He forced himself to put away the bitter memories and focus on what Darius was saying.

' … so, while we send out to the furthest reaches

of our Empire and gather our forces once more – and this time our numbers will be so overwhelming we will drown the barbarians in their own blood – Axtya has suggested another possibility, a way to ensure our victory. And that is why I have summoned you.' Darius leaned forward and laid a hand on the young noble's shoulder. It was a great honour to be touched by the King of Kings.

'Go with Axtya now and he will explain as he sees fit. It is my explicit command that you follow any and all of his instructions as if they came from me. Do you understand?' Adarfiroz was taken aback to be put at this unknown man's beck and call, but bowed and murmured the appropriate words. With that the audience was at an end and Axtya took Adarfiroz's arm and guided him out of the hall.

Afghanistan, 333 BC

They had ridden for many days now through this land of desert and rocks and Adarfiroz knew his men had begun cursing him and calling him a fool behind his back. Only weeks ago they had still hailed him as the great warrior they had sworn to follow to the ends of the earth. Well, he thought grimly, all he had done was take them at their word. His dark brooding eyes never ceased scanning his surroundings and he glanced back at his men riding sullenly across the dusty wasteland. Only forty left. Most had died at Issus, and five more had expired along the way. He licked his parched lips. Without water they would soon all be food for the vultures.

He mentally cursed Alexander and all he stood for – his arrogance, brutality and above all for bringing with him the Greek juggernaut that was obliterating their ancient culture. His gaze lingered on the old man. The soldiers hated him almost as much as Alexander for being the cause of their current hardship, but had grudgingly come to respect the fact that he kept up with the best of them, never complaining and seemingly untouched by the rigours of their journey.

After the audience with Darius Axtya had taken him to his chambers in the palace. Once servants had brought food and wine Adarfiroz leaned back and regarded his host.

'So, what is this plan that has persuaded Darius to put me at your disposal? You have satisfied my thirst and hunger, and now it is time to satisfy my curiosity.' The old man nodded and reached into one of the many pockets in his robes and held up a small golden idol with ruby eyes. Adarfiroz raised his eyebrows enquiringly. The old man got up and stood next to him.

'I beg you to indulge me, noble Adarfiroz,' he said. 'But I have certain ... abilities that will make things clearer than mere words ever could. May I lay a hand on your brow?' Adarfiroz was perplexed by this strange request but nodded impatiently.

'Yes, yes, if you think it is really necessary.' Axtya held the idol in one hand and laid his hand lightly on Adarfiroz's forehead.

'Allow yourself to relax, please. Close your eyes. Clear your mind and let your muscles be at rest.' Adarfiroz did his best, but a part of his mind was impatient with this mumbo-jumbo. The old man's voice was soothing, though, and he felt himself drifting into something like a doze.

All at once he was on a wide plain and the Greek army was spread out before him. A shadow blotted out the sun as a great yellow dragon soared over him and dived shrieking into the Greek army, its huge teeth slashing through their ranks and swinging an immense spiked tail that hurled broken men through the air like scattered seed.

He opened his eyes, his chest tight with tension and found the old man staring at him intently.

'I too have seen this vision, Lord, and I know you have seen a great serpent from the lands to the South from which this idol comes. I have studied these visions and believe we may summon the creature to wreak revenge on the Greeks.' Adarfiroz shook his head to clear it and goggled at him.

'What? This is the plan with which you have persuaded the King? Some mythical monster that will defeat the Greeks? Ahura Mazda save us. We are lost indeed!' Axtya regarded him steadily and carefully placed the idol on the table between them.

'Before the battle of Issus I spoke with many men from all over the Empire. One of them hailed from the land of the Afghans and was something of a shaman amongst his people. He had many of the same gifts I have been blessed with, and had seen his future and knew he was going to die. He gave me this, his most treasured possession, to keep safe and return to the land of his fathers.' He pointed at the idol.

'It is called Zhun and has always been linked to the great serpents. They say that in the land of the Afghans the temples to Zhun are built on mounds that are the carcasses of these immense creatures. And I believe it is enabling us to see what may be done.'

Adarfiroz gazed into the unyielding eyes of the Mage and slumped back into his chair. *Why not,* he thought. *My home is gone – I heard of its destruction after the battle. Why not indeed? One last adventure … and if it were to be true … oh, Ahura Mazda! If it were to be true …*

Afghanistan, 2010

Alan Bishop hated Afghanistan. He hated everything about it. The fanatical Taliban, the heat, the dust, the way everything was crumbling, living like tramps in the sand-bagged abandoned building that had become their outpost and last but not least the not inconsiderable chance of getting killed or wounded. He was 21 years old and had been enthusiastic and gung-ho when he arrived and that had lasted until his first engagement with the enemy.

His platoon had been on patrol and the village seemed deserted. The only sound was from sheets of plastic flapping in the wind. Like a ghost town in a Western movie. Except here the Indians had Kalashnikovs.

One minute it was eerie silence and the next there were bullets everywhere, thudding into the mud-brick walls and making high-pitched *zipping* sounds as they passed through the air. Two of his platoon were hit but then they got the LMG – Light Machine Gun - to bear and in minutes the Taliban were history. One of his two wounded comrades made it, the other didn't. He remembered walking over to the five bearded, blood-spattered corpses after it was all over and looking down at them and stepping back not because it sickened him but recoiling from the wave of hate that somehow still radiated from their lifeless forms.

So, two months later, another mate dead and he was doing the same bloody thing yet again, like that movie – what was it ? *Ground Hog Day*, that was it. Christ. Less than four months to go. He couldn't wait for his six month tour to be over so he could get out of this shit-hole.

It had all started so well. The basic training in

England, more training in Kenya – it had all seemed like the adventure of a lifetime. Then the eight hour flight to Kandahar and his first taste of Afghanistan. Then the helicopter flight to Helmand province. And then the reality.

He had a lot of time on his hands and sometimes thought of the family tradition that somewhere far back in their history there had been an exotic ancestor, generally thought to have come from this part of the world. His father had told him about it, clearly not believing it but passing on the titbit of family lore as his father had done before him, and enjoying his mother's tight-lipped rejection of the idea as fanciful and "complete rubbish."

He sighed and hunkered down behind the sandbags on the roof of the abandoned police station that was their base and looked up at the ink-black night sky spray-painted with stars. He closed his eyes and prayed to any deity that might happen to be listening to just let him get through this and get home. And ignoring the uncomfortable, very small part of him that felt as if he *had* come home.

Afghanistan, 333 BC

They found themselves in a broad valley, a little less arid than the land they had slogged through for what seemed like forever. They approached a figure surrounded by a small herd of goats and Adarfiroz raised his hand to halt the column of riders.

The goatherd was small and wiry and burnt dark brown by prolonged exposure to the sun and elements and regarded them warily. Axtya rode forward and greeted him in a language Adarfiroz couldn't understand. After a few minutes of animated conversation the goatherd pointed emphatically towards the foot of the mountains on one side of the valley. The Mage rode back and pointed in the same direction.

'He confirms that the home of the man who gave me the idol is a village a couple of hours ride over there. He was well-known and well-respected, it would appear. Shall we?' Without waiting for a response the Mage set off. Adarfiroz signalled to his men and they trotted after him.

The village was more like a small town, fortified with thick mud-brick walls and an ancient iron-bound gate. Once again Axtya's words seemed to have a positive effect and they were ushered in by some rough-looking guards and taken to what was clearly the principal building. Their horses and his men were led away and the two of them entered a long, smoky room at whose end sat a hawk-faced man with eyes like black marbles and an equally black beard who was obviously the local chieftain. He gestured to them to sit on carpets strewn about the edge of the room, where they joined half a dozen other men who could have been the chieftain's brothers, all attired like their leader in long, dun-coloured robes. After the inevitable offering of a fiery spirit and sweetmeats, Axtya began talking.

At one point he produced the golden idol and a murmur ran around the room. A meal of roast lamb and unleavened bread followed and then the travellers were each shown to small cell-like rooms with a pallet and a jug of water and left to their own devices. Adarfiroz went out to check on his men and finding they had been well looked after returned to his room. Although it was late, Axtya was waiting for him and swiftly outlined the gist of what had been said earlier.

Even this remote valley had heard of the great battles and Persian defeats by Alexander. They were grieved to hear of the death of their shaman, who was apparently regarded as exceptionally powerful and held in great reverence. The fact that Axtya was a Mage and now possessed the idol seemed to have conferred some of that awe on him, and for that reason as well as the fact the he represented the Empire that still ruled them, the tribal leaders had agreed to help them in their quest.

Axtya stopped talking in mid-sentence and put his hand to his lips, dousing the guttering oil lamp that was their only illumination. Enough moonlight filtered through a tiny window set high in the wall to see the door open slowly. A shrouded figure slipped in, closing it after them. Adarfiroz seized the intruder in an iron grip pinioning the arms as Axtya ran to his room and returned with a lit oil lamp and pulled away the cloth shrouding the intruder's head. Adarfiroz gasped as a young woman was revealed and as he released her his hands inadvertently brushed soft, full breasts.

She was raven-haired and beautiful with big liquid eyes and a full, sensual mouth and Adarfiroz couldn't take his eyes off her. Axtya spoke to her and to his surprise she replied in halting Dari, the lingua franca of the Persian Empire. She was the dead shaman's sister, and wanted to know the circumstances of her brother's death. Axtya gently related how he had fallen in battle and she covered her face with her hands. They waited until she had collected herself and her gaze met the young noble's and time seemed to stand still as they gazed at each other. Finally she turned and spoke to Axtya, who had busied himself re-lighting the other lamp. He turned to Adarfiroz with a quizzical expression.

'Now that I have told her what she wants to know, it seems she wants to be left alone with you. Have a care, my Lord. I do not know these people's customs. But I suspect that a young unmarried woman spending time alone with a strange man might prove … less than popular!' He gave a little bow and withdrew, closing the door behind him.

The two young people looked at each other again and as before time seemed to hold its breath. Finally Adarfiroz opened his mouth to ask what she wanted with him but she reached out and put a finger to his lips. As if in a dream he drew her closer and they kissed and he felt the heat of her body against his and they sank onto the pallet. And then somehow their clothes were no longer on their bodies but strewn about the room and they were together, mouth against mouth, skin against skin and the rest of the world faded away and there was just the two of them becoming one.

Afghanistan, 2010

Alan sat in the Chinook with six other soldiers. The doors were open, the noise from the two rotors was deafening, and the almost featureless sand-coloured landscape seemed to go on forever. All at once there was a series of loud metallic pings and he saw a hole appear in the floor between his feet.

'Shit!' he yelled. 'We're under fire, looks like from right below us!' As he spoke the helicopter veered off to one side like a startled gazelle. Over the next few minutes it swung this way and that, gaining speed all the time. Alan unclasped his belt and lurched towards the cockpit. What he saw was not good. The co-pilot was slumped forward, motionless. One of the pilot's arms hung uselessly by his side, the sleeve drenched in blood while he fought to control the machine with the other.

Alan leaped forward and after a struggle managed to unbuckle the co-pilot's belt and pull his body from its seat. He sat down and turned to the pilot.

'Quick! Tell me what I can do to help!' The pilot slowly turned to him and to his horror Alan saw his plastic visor was shattered and that half his jaw was gone. His eyes rolled up and he fell lifelessly to one side. Alan turned helplessly to the controls. The helicopter's engines were screaming now and the ground was a blur unravelling at frightening speed. He gritted his teeth and gripped the controls.

'You can do this. You can do this,' he repeated under his breath. For some time he managed to just hold the controls steady and speed along in a more or less straight line. His first attempt to move the stick sent the helicopter into a sickening, yawing dive and he pulled back very, very slowly and miraculously the dive flattened. But now they were dangerously close to the ground and Alan looked up and saw a hill directly in front of them. He yanked the stick towards him and for a moment thought he was going to make it. The Chinook seemed to stand almost motionless on its tail, the engines screamed and metal shrieked as a rotor broke away and he remembered nothing else.

*

The first thing Alan noticed when consciousness returned was the pain. He hurt all over and every movement seemed to produce jolts of agony. He lay motionless and after a while the pain began to subside. Very carefully and gingerly he levered himself up to a sitting position and groaned at what he saw.

What was left of the Chinook was a blazing pyre and parts of it were scattered all around. There were no bodies visible and Alan could only assume they were still inside the inferno. He managed to stand up and groggily checked himself. His combat fatigues were torn and filthy. The back of his head hurt like hell and his hand came away bloody when he touched it, but when he gritted his teeth and probed with his fingers his skull seemed to be intact. He felt bruised all over and one knee felt like it was on fire every time he moved. He forced himself to limp closer to the helicopter but could see nothing through the flames and the smoke. He started feeling dizzy and sat down abruptly.

When he awoke again dusk was falling fast as it always did in this part of the world. The fire in the Chinook had died down and he approached it with a sinking heart. When he peered in he saw a blackened cavern of twisted metal with indistinct shapes that had once been his comrades, neatly strapped in a row.

He started wondering why nobody had come to check on them yet and it struck him for the first time that he was utterly alone in a hostile country. With a sudden sense of urgency he started circling the wreck, searching through the debris. By the time it was dark he had collected a pile of salvaged items and was sorting through them under a rising moon that was almost as bright as day.

He felt he had been incredibly lucky, quite apart from surviving the crash. It seemed that the impact had thrown out almost anything that wasn't tied down. He had a choice of two Heckler and Koch SA 80 rifles, ammunition pouches, a medical kit and ration packs. There was even a chemical water heater, but no water. He closed his eyes and visualised the briefing map. If they had stayed on course the way back should be almost due west. He pulled out his compass and squinted at it in the moonlight. He collected everything in one pouch, picked up a rifle and started limping across a barren landscape strewn with low hills.

*

Exhaustion and the pain from his knee finally made him stop. He settled himself by a clump of small thorny bushes at the foot of one of the innumerable small hills that would at least give him some cover and hopefully some shade when the sun came up and was asleep in seconds.

When he awoke the sun was already well above the distant mountains and he could feel the temperature creeping up. He heard voices and froze, then very, very slowly picked up his rifle and checked the magazine. The voices were definitely not English or American and they seemed to be coming from the other side of the little hill. Then the unintelligible words were punctuated by a cry of pain. In the end his need to know overcame his instinct to stay put and he started inching his way up the slope until he could peer down the other side.

Two Afghans stood over a third man lying on the ground before them. They were heavily bearded and had Kalashnikovs slung over their shoulders and one of them was in the act of bringing down a leather whip on the prostrate figure. It connected with a sickening *thwack* and the victim screamed. He was an old man, thin as a whippet and wearing an unusual long white robe with strange symbols worked around the sleeves.

The other Taliban (Alan had no doubt that was what they were) kicked him viciously in the ribs and the two men laughed as he groaned and writhed in pain. They seemed to become bored with this and unslung their weapons and pointed them at the old man. Their intention was unmistakeable and Alan acted without thinking. He steadied the SA80, flicked the selector to single rounds, aimed and fired. The first Taliban's head seemed to disintegrate and as the other man froze in slack-jawed amazement he carefully placed two rounds in his chest.

He was certain they were dead but nonetheless held his weapon at the ready and prodded each of the two corpses to make sure before turning to the old man who was scrabbling for a wooden staff and laboriously getting to his feet. Alan helped him up and he looked down at the bodies before dismissing them and turning back to Alan.

'English?' he asked. Alan nodded and the old man's leathery brown face broke into a smile, revealing a remarkably white set of teeth.

'Thank you for disposing of this vermin so efficiently. Your timing was impeccable and I am deeply in your debt. May I ask what you are doing here? It is rather in the middle of nowhere. I have always liked that expression and it describes where we are perfectly. I am Jawid.' He held out his hand and Alan shook it. Jawid beckoned to him and after collecting his pouch Alan walked with him between the hills and told him how he came to be there. They passed a battered pickup truck listing heavily to one side.

'They were lost, you see, and then their vehicle broke an axle. And then unfortunately they chanced upon me.' He saw Alan forming a question and smiled.

'What had I done to offend them? Ah well. That is a long story and we do not have far to go.' They walked a little further until they reached a long, low hill. It had a brooding, unsettling presence and between some boulders at its foot Jawid led him into a cave. Alan was astonished to find it furnished with carpets and a divan and tables and chairs. Jawid sat him down and poured him a glass of cool water that Alan gulped down greedily, soothing his parched throat. All at once tiredness overwhelmed him and he fell into a deep sleep.

The old man sat and looked at his guest for a long time.

'Can it be?' he said to himself. 'Is it possible? Can he be the one? *An Englishman?*' He stood over Alan's inert form and gently placed a hand on his head.

Moments later he nodded. Yes, it was true. After all this time. Now there were things this young man needed to know. Perhaps not consciously, but subtly placed where he could recall them when the need arose.

Afghanistan, 333 BC

Her name was Behrukh and she was waiting for them as dawn broke. She looked magnificent astride her white horse and Adarfiroz thought he had never seen anything so beautiful in his life. A white goat was tethered to her pommel on a long rope.

'She will take us where we need to go,' said Axtya. 'You are fortunate indeed not to be suffering a prolonged and exquisitely painful end at the hands of her male relatives, but it seems that those of this particular bloodline are free of all normal social restraints.' The three of them set their horses in motion and the soldiers mounted up and followed.

They rode for most of the day through a land of low hills and ridges until Behrukh reined in her horse and pointed at a long ridge that petered out to ground level at both ends. She regarded them seriously.

'Those are the remains of Aži Zairita, the yellow dragon. With the right incantations and offerings he can be summoned. The spells exist but nobody knows whether it has ever actually been done. Old man, I need your assistance. Are you sure this is what you want?'

'It is what we came for,' said Adarfiroz and she nodded.

'So be it.'

The three of them climbed up the ridge, dragging the protesting goat with them. When they reached the top Adarfiroz could see that to a superstitious mind the ridge could indeed look like the remains of some immense beast, the rocky outcrops along the top like enormous vertebrae. His musings were interrupted as Axtya took out the golden idol and Behrukh took his hand and the three of them held it, their hands touching and overlapping. She closed her eyes and began muttering unintelligible phrases, at the same time drawing a long knife from her robes. As she uttered the last word the knife flashed out and cut the unfortunate goat's throat. Its blood fountained onto the parched yellow stone, glistening and shockingly bright crimson in the harsh sunlight.

The ground shook beneath their feet and Behrukh and Axtya grimly hung onto the golden idol while she started chanting under her breath, the same names over and over again. *Zhun. Aži Zairita. Zhun. Aži Zairita. Zhun. Aži Zairita …*

The rumbling tremor subsided and all was quiet again. Behrukh turned to him and handed him the idol.

'You are now the custodian of Zhun, and Aži Zairita is confined within. But only one of the bloodline that has served Zhun from time immemorial can command him. So I must come with you and when our son is born he will take on the mantle.' Adarfiroz's eyes widened.

'Our son?' Behrukh smiled and he felt himself go weak at the knees. It was as if all the best days of his life had been combined and concentrated into that one moment. She nodded, still smiling.

'Yes, my beloved. Our child grows within me as we speak. A child of power, and of love. Are you happy?' He nodded speechlessly and took her hand.

Afghanistan, 2010

Jawid walked with him for what seemed like hours before he pointed and Alan saw the highway running like a grey ribbon across the featureless plain in the distance. The old man held out his hand and Alan shook it.

'Go with the Gods, my friend, and as a token of my gratitude please take this.' He handed him a soft leather pouch and Alan opened it and stared at the golden idol with ruby eyes in his hand.

'Jawid! I can't possibly ... ' the old man laid a hand on his arm and all at once Alan was suffused with a sense of how right it was to have the ... whatever it was.

'It is a representation of Zhun,' the old man said carefully. 'Please heed my words – from now on you must always keep him with you. Always, no matter what. Do you understand?' Alan nodded dumbly. His conscious mind didn't understand what the old man was saying, but at the same time he somehow, weirdly, knew he was right and that he would do just that. Jawid nodded, smiled, clapped him on the back and started walking back the way they had come.

Alan stood there for a long time watching him get smaller and smaller and when the old man didn't turn to wave or look back in his direction, he shook himself and headed for the highway.

Less than an hour passed before he saw two approaching dots that rapidly grew and resolved themselves into Warrior infantry vehicles that clanked to a noisy halt when they saw him standing in the road.

A couple of hours later he was back at base. The debriefing went on for some time and he omitted all mention of the old man and the idol nestling heavily in a pocket of his fatigues. He wasn't quite sure why he did so, but somehow knew it was best to keep all of that strange episode secret. When he was done he headed straight for his bunk and fell into a deep sleep.

Afghanistan, 333 BC

They had been riding for days. They emerged from a valley and reined in their horses. Ranged across their path was a small army of five hundred or so foot soldiers led by a small group of riders. The leader called a halt and came cantering towards them with two fierce-looking companions. The man himself was a barrel-chested swarthy individual with gaudy armour that groaned at the seams in an heroic attempt to contain his considerable girth. They rode up very close almost to touching distance before coming to a stop. The fat one's smile was confident and oily as he surveyed the small band and when his eyes glided lingeringly over Behrukh like the caress of a sweaty hand Adarfiroz forced himself not to react. The man finally turned his eyes to him and nodded.

'Lord Adarfiroz, is it not?' He nodded and remained silent.

'Good, good,' said the man. 'My name is Morad and I am satrap of this region. Where are you travelling to?

'Perhaps you could first inform us how you know my name and why you have stopped us,' Adarfiroz said evenly. 'We are on a mission under the direct command of Darius, King of Kings. What is your business with us?' Morad's eyes again slid lasciviously over Behrukh and the young Persian exerted all his will power to remain calm.

'Never mind how I know,' said Morad. 'Things have changed since you left Persepolis, my young friend. The great Lord Alexander will soon have possession of all the Empire and those who are wise enough to be reeds that bend with the wind will not break, rather they will flourish. If you surrender to me peaceably I will deliver you to my new master. He has been known to be merciful to those who have not offended him directly, so you will have a sporting chance. As for you, my dear,' he smiled wetly at Behrukh, 'you I will take care of … personally!'

There was a swish of metal and a blur of movement and Morad's head went spinning into the dust, his face an almost comical rictus of surprise. The severed neck spurted blood and then the lifeless body sagged and toppled off his horse. Before the two lieutenants had time to react they too were dead and the three companions looked at each other. A roar of outrage rose from the massed ranks of soldiers in the distance and they turned their horses, calling to their men to retreat.

In their headlong rush they galloped into a valley and to their horror saw that it narrowed into a vertical cliff face. It was a dead end.

'We will die here, I think,' said Adarfiroz. He and his men formed a line and waited. Soon Morad's soldiers were thronging the mouth of the valley and running full tilt towards them. Adarfiroz took Behrukh's hand and kissed it, looking deep into her eyes.

'It only remains to die like men,' he said. 'Swear to me you will use your knife on yourself before they get to you.' She said something softly which he took to be her promise and raised his sword.

'Chaaarge!' he yelled at the top of his voice and his small band of riders thundered towards their pursuers.

'Not this time, my love,' said Behrukh softly and laid her hand on his arm. Adarfiroz sagged and she and Axtya pressed their mounts against his and held him upright. She looked at the old man and he nodded grimly. With one hand she retrieved the idol of Zhun and began murmuring incantations. Just as Adarfiroz's handful of men reached the opposing force the ground trembled and everyone paused. With a loud tearing sound and an ear-splitting clap like thunder the air seemed to part.

A vast yellow figure materialised in mid-air and with a roar that brought rocks tumbling down the sides of the valley it flicked an enormous tail from side to side and dove towards the mass of men on the valley floor.

Afghanistan, 2010

Alan sat behind the wall of sandbags on the flat roof of their base, scanning the featureless surrounding landscape with night vision goggles. His mind was only half on the job at hand. He just couldn't stop thinking about the idol of Zhun heavy in his pocket and had the constant unsettling feeling that there were things he ought to remember but that remained maddeningly just out of reach. A movement caught his eye. Yes, there was definitely someone or something moving out there. There was another one … and another …

Like stars coming out at night one heat signature after another popped into view until there was a whole ragged line of them moving stealthily towards the base. He kicked his corporal who had dozed off.

'Jonesy! For fuck's sake wake up! We're being attacked – there's God know how many of the buggers out there, I'm seeing more all the time!' Jonesy scrambled down the rickety ladder and ran around waking the others. By the time the two platoons were up and in position Alan thought there must be over a hundred, maybe many more. And they were getting uncomfortably close.

Alan signalled to the two men manning the GPMG – General Purpose Machine Gun.

'Hold your fire,' he hissed. 'Let them get a little closer. On my signal.' As he dropped his hand and the machine gun burst into chattering action he heard the *whump whump* of mortars in the distance and the shells landed a few feet from the compound wall, showering them with dust.

It was like a scene from hell. Noise and dust were everywhere, the chattering and barking of gunfire, the firing and explosion of mortar shells, the screaming of commands and of the wounded. The fire they were returning was lessening and Alan realized that one man after another was being put out of action and they were in imminent danger of being overrun. The GPMG was still firing but there were just too many of them. Alan popped his head above the parapet enough to scan the area with his night vision goggles and was horrified at the number of eerily glowing figures still advancing on them.

The radio operator had sent a distress call but with all the luck in the world it would be ten to fifteen minutes before air support arrived and a lot longer for reinforcements. He didn't think they had five minutes let alone ten. A grenade landed by the machine gun crew and a moment later they were dead and Alan was flat on his back, his ears ringing and his head buzzing. He could hear the wild cries of the attackers and they sounded horribly close.

Without really knowing what he was doing he reached into his fatigues pocket and brought out the idol of Zhun. As if he were observing a stranger he heard himself uttering strange phrases and even though he couldn't actually understand the words he somehow knew what they meant and what to say.

The whole building shook and there was a puzzled lull in the frenzy of the battle. With what sounded like a clap of thunder a vast shape blotted out the stars and the triumphant shouting of the Taliban turned into shrieks of fear. He poked his head above the parapet again and stared disbelievingly at a giant yellow monster that swooped down on the tightly packed attackers and plucked them up with a mouth the size of a bus and swept across them with an enormous spiked tail that sent them spinning brokenly through the air like ninepins. In minutes there were no more heat signatures showing on his goggles and he tore them off. The thing, whatever it was - *Aži Zairita* he whispered without knowing why - wasn't registering either.

He stood up painfully and not a hundred yards away an enormous head raised itself and stared back at him. Human body parts dangled from sabre-like teeth the size of elephant tusks and two eyes like burning coals bored into him. It looked around and turned its attention back to him, taking a huge step that halved the distance between them.

He clutched the idol and again from nowhere words were coming out of his mouth, ancient, repetitive, authoritative and irresistible. The creature threw back its head and roared, a sound of such primitive and other-worldly fury he felt his legs give way. There was another thunderous clap and it disappeared as if it had never been.

Afghanistan, 333 BC

The three of them sat motionless on their horses. The animals were hard to control, panting and skittering from side to side with terrified, rolling eyes. The monster was gone, sent back to wherever it came from, but they were the only ones left alive. Everything that had been alive on the valley floor was now dead, friend and foe alike. Tearing their eyes away from the carnage they looked wordlessly at each other.

'We cannot let this thing loose on the world again,' said Adarfiroz. 'Darius is not the man to vanquish Alexander and I fear our cause is lost.' He held out his hands, one to Behrukh and one to Axtya.

'Let us return to your home, my love. And there you, Axtya can be the custodian of this terrible object. You, who knows what it can do and how to make it do it, but whose voice it will not obey. And you, my love, who also knows but can make it do your bidding. Let us live the rest of our lives in peace and hope this is never unleashed on the world again.'

They nodded, clasped their hands in silent communion, and set off back the way they had come.

Ministry
of Defence

Defence Intelligence & Security Centre, Chicksands

20th September 2010

BY HAND

TOP SECRET

Delivery : sealed pouch by courier with armed escort
From :   OC / DISC (Afghanistan Section)
To :   The Prime Minister - <u>FOR YOUR EYES ONLY</u>

Dear Prime Minister

Further to your request for a detailed account of the
events at Outpost 655 in Afghanistan earlier this year,
please find attached my report along with eye-witness
statements from the survivors of the attack and our
assessment of those statements and the physical
evidence

Ref Section 1.0 Summary of Physical Evidence

Ref Section 2.0 Summary of Witness Statements

Section 1 - Summary of Physical Evidence

British casualties both dead and wounded all show "normal" battlefield trauma, i.e. injuries from small arms, mortars and grenades.

Enemy casualties are more problematic. First, there were no survivors, which of itself is highly unusual given the circumstances. While here too there is some "normal" battlefield trauma, mainly from the defensive GPMG (which by the way proved very effective) the over 200 bodies identified have injuries which have defied analysis. An exact number is hard to ascertain as there are numerous body parts without bodies, and conversely bodies missing body parts. The physical separation appears to have been either by being torn apart by some massive force or slashed by some very large sharp object.

In the absence of any precedent extensive autopsies have failed to provide any credible explanation and the matter remains unresolved.

Section 2 - Summary of Witness Statements

As can be seen from the attached Witness Statements, there is a considerable degree of confusion and little coherence or consistency in the survivor's accounts. Only Sergeant Alan Bishop has steadfastly maintained his account with no variations despite its fantastic nature. His delusion appears to centre on an ancient golden idol and yet he is singularly unforthcoming as to how it came into his possession.

See Witness Statement # 6 appended

Analysis by Sir Michael Hargreaves, the leading expert on Middle Eastern Antiquities at the British Museum (*copy of his signed Official Secrets Act statement attached*) suggests that it is from the region in question and is a minimum of 5,000 years old and possibly much more. He believes it to be a representation of Zhun, a pre-Islamic cult figure. Sir Michael states that there is evidence to suggest that, based on the worship of a golden idol with ruby eyes, the cult of Zhun survived the arrival of Islam. The idol's temple was supposedly located "by the vertebra of a giant reptile" believed to be that of a dragon. The priests of Zhun were credited with shaman-like abilities including the power to control demons and other supernatural forces and being able to both heal and harm people.

How Sergeant Bishop (whose education did not proceed beyond GCSE standard - *see attached Personnel File*) came by this esoteric knowledge and why he came to incorporate it into what we believe to be an extreme case of post-traumatic stress disorder remains an unanswered question.

On a personal note, I hope to see you both at Binky's this weekend.

James

Ministry
of Defence

Defence Intelligence & Security Centre, Chicksands

15th October 2010

BY HAND

TOP SECRET

Dear Prime Minister

I thought I ought to update you personally on developments re the Outpost 655 affair. I should mention that no official record of these developments has been made and I would strongly suggest that you personally destroy this note once read.

It would appear that an unknown individual managed to gain access to the detention facility where Sergeant Bishop was being held and that they then somehow managed to evade the guards and disappear. We are obviously looking into it but as with the Outpost 655 surviving troops' statements, the NCO in charge and the guards have no coherent explanation to offer.

Further, the golden idol itself has inexplicably disappeared from the British Museum's vaults and again there is no explanation for how this occurred.

If I may make a personal suggestion, it might be best all round if we regard this whole affair as a sleeping dog to be let lie.

James

Michael Anderson

 Prime Minister's Office
10 Downing Street

From the Prime Minister's Office

11th November 2010

BY HAND

Dear James

Re the Outpost 655 business, thank you for your reports and recommendations. I must say I find the whole thing damned odd, but have been rather busy of late dealing with our European friends and other matters (as I am sure you have gathered from the newspapers!)

By the way, a chum of mine at MI5 mentioned a sighting of someone matching the description of your missing sergeant in Afghanistan! Looks like your chaps missed a trick on that one! Can't win them all, eh!

With that sentiment in mind I quite agree that in the absence of substantive fresh developments we should close the file on this one.

Looking forward to seeing at the shoot at Lord Harberry's – given the size of your bag last year perhaps you should bring along one of those GPMGs!

Kind Regards and keep up the good work

D.

A Place Of Her Own

Die Gedanken sind frei, wer kann sie erraten, sie fliegen vorbei
wie nächtliche Schatten.
(Thoughts are free, who can guess them? They fly past like
nocturnal shadows)

German song, circa 1780, author unknown

I opened my eyes and wished I hadn't. I'd forgotten to pull down the blinds last night and it was a sunny morning in London – a rather cruel trick of fate to inflict such a rare occurrence on me just now, I thought. The sun's rays were like hot pokers in my eyes and I seemed to have forgotten anything that happened last night. I let my brain settle down for a while and when the pounding became bearable pushed myself up to a sitting position and let myself go slack, exhausted by the effort.

Through half-open eyes I glanced at the bed and saw that only my side had been slept on, and that I was still wearing my socks and chinos but thankfully not my shoes. So it seemed likely that for once I had been alone when I got home, whenever that was. I sat there avoiding movement while the different parts of my body started getting reacquainted and conferred about maybe getting together and working as a team again. The thought of coffee entered my mind and seemed like a very clever and important thing to focus on.

A little later I was in the kitchen, wincing as the kettle got up a head of steam, making the angry grumbling popping sound of water meeting hot metal. Could we really have reached the 21st Century without anybody inventing a silent kettle? It seemed unlikely and I made a mental note to check it out.

I'm always making mental notes about things, I can't help it. I also always mean to follow them up, but somehow never get around to it. I sat at the small kitchen table and the first sip of hot coffee seared its way down my throat. I made a long *aaaaah* sound, part pleasure and part pain. I was idly wondering about the relative proportions of the two sensations when I started getting this weird fuzzy feeling in my head.

Now you may have deduced from my lack of surprise at my condition that this was not the first time I had felt like this. Not by a long shot. A very, very long shot. So I knew what a hangover felt like. I was an expert on every nuance and combination of its symptoms. The queasiness. The dry mouth. The strange way floors behaved when you tried to stand up. The pain behind the eyeballs, quite distinct from the pain over the eyes or at the back of the head. You would have thought they would coordinate in some way, these various pains, what with being in the same body and all. But no, the fiendish stabbing pain behind the eyeballs led a separate life to the dull drumbeat in the main part of my head, each one single-mindedly sending out its own particular brand of agony, gleefully unpredictable and unsyncopated. Stab stab thud stab thud thud. I groaned and drank more coffee.

So this unusual feeling took me by surprise and worried me because I didn't recognise it. It was an unwelcome intruder, like a banjo in a string quartet. It was as if a mist was drifting into my head and slowly filling it, making the other stuff recede. Not that that was necessarily a bad thing. But I didn't seem to have any control over it and there was something about it that made me uneasy. Something insistent and frightening and I wanted it to go away but it wouldn't. I found myself back in the bedroom hunting for my shoes and picking up my jacket and before I knew it I was on the pavement outside my apartment building.

The sun was blinding and painful and I pawed at

my jacket pocket and sighed with relief when I found my sunglasses and managed to slip them on without stabbing my eyeballs. My other hand went out in a sort of shaky Nazi salute and a black cab drew up. Why had I stopped it? I had no idea and by now I had a sinking feeling in the pit of my stomach. What the hell was happening to me? I didn't seem to know what I was doing from one moment to the next.

I leaned into the open window, staggering slightly. The driver was bull-necked with a shaved head and an earring, and recoiled with a wrinkled nose in an unexpected show of sensitivity. I suppose not brushing my teeth or showering might have had something to do with it.

'St. Martha's hospital,' I said and fell rather than sat in the back, clumsily pulling the door closed behind me.

'Right you are, Guv,' he said and we jerked away into the traffic and for a moment I thought my head was going to fall off. Each bump in the road was exaggerated rather than softened by the taxi's non-existent suspension and sent a wave of nausea through me. It was as much the fear of facing the formidable-looking driver as anything else that stopped me from finding out what I had had for dinner last night.

I have no idea how long it took before we lurched to a halt in front of a stern Victorian red brick building. I peered owlishly out of the window and regarded the brushed steel letters that spelled out St. Martha's Hospital. I was idly imagining the committee meeting that had decided on signage so wildly out of keeping with the rest of the building when the cabbie's voice penetrated my reverie.

'You all right Guv? Guv! That's fifteen pounds 80 pence. Hello? Anybody home in there?' I shook myself, dug out my wallet and stuffed a twenty pound note in his hand and told him to keep the change. He became considerably friendlier after that and told me to have a nice day. I felt absurdly grateful but had a feeling it was not going to be a nice day at all. Just a hunch. I stood on the pavement and watched him shoot off into the traffic without indicating and turned around to face the building.

I somehow made it up the steps – there seemed to be an awful lot of them – and my head was swimming by the time I had gone through the swooshing automatic doors and entered the blessedly quiet interior. I let the tastefully soothing blue and green decor calm me and took a few steps forward and tripped over the leg of a chair – they protruded slightly, a bloody silly design. A passing nurse in a blue and white striped smock stopped and gently took my arm.

'Are you all right, sir? Do you require assistance?' I hate unnecessarily long words in everyday conversation, but had enough sense to stop my instinctive retort of *No, but I do need help* ... I assured her I was okay and she went off reluctantly, casting a couple of speculative looks at me before dismissing me and disappearing around a corner.

I stood there helplessly, swaying slightly as my brain tried to coordinate concentrated thinking and overall body control. What was I doing here? Now what? Why the hell ...

Third floor. Room 327. It was as if somebody had whispered the words in my ear and I spun around, not an easy manoeuvre for someone in my condition,

I can tell you. When I saw there was nobody within twenty feet of me I steadied myself and walked towards the sign that said LIFTS.

The wait seemed interminable and so did the agonisingly slow ascent. I thought about how easy it would be to murder the owner of the condescending voice that accompanied my journey.

Doors closing. Doors closing. First Floor. Doors opening. Doors opening. Doors closing. Doors closing. Second Floor. Doors opening. Doors opening. Doors closing. Doors closing. Third Floor. Doors opening …

I was through them in a flash, or as close to a flash as I was able to manage, and saw a nurse's station. A thin woman with short hair wearing the hospital's blue and white stripes was impatiently tapping her keyboard and glancing at an open file and muttering irritably to herself. She seemed too absorbed in her task to register my presence and in any case I had absolutely no idea what to say to her. I noticed that the doors to my right were all numbered in cheery yellow plastic and kept walking.

320, 321 … I arrived at 327 and decided there was no point in knocking and opened the door, closing it behind me and leaning against it to catch my breath. The blinds were drawn and the pale flecked violet floor coordinated nicely with two visitor's chairs in a muted purple fabric. The rest was clinically white, as was the bed, a complicated tubular metal contraption of levers and pedals and collapsible side bars.

On it lay a figure on its back, head swathed in bandages and arms by its side as if standing to attention while lying down. There were two distinct bumps under the sheets in the chest area and I cleverly deduced it was a woman. The fact that they rose and fell rhythmically led me to the further brilliant conclusion that she was breathing. Tubes ran from her arms and nose to various silent but hopefully vigilant machines.

I stepped closer and stood by her side, looking down with the question *why am I here* circling around my brain like a ball on a roulette table after the croupier has called *rien ne va plus*. Only it never settled in a slot. One of her eyes was bruised and turning interesting shades of yellow at the edges. There was something about her ... my heart started beating faster and I didn't know why and I pulled up a chair and sat down abruptly, my legs suddenly rubbery. It was only when I saw her profile from that angle that the penny finally dropped.

Nicola. Nicky. I shook myself as if I was covered in something unpleasant like cobwebs and wanted to shake them off. It couldn't be. But that profile ... the perfect retroussé nose, the full lips, the fine, sculpted eyebrows, the cheekbones that I always thought hinted at some Slavic ancestry lurking in the family tree ... oh my God. I looked down at her hand and my heart was pounding like a jackhammer. There it was. The thin little band of white gold with microscopic diamonds that had taken every penny I could beg, borrow or steal at the time.

Her voice in my ear. *I will always wear this. Always.* My hand crept towards hers and took her cool fingers in mine. My fingertips touched the tiny stones, half expecting them to be a figment of my imagination and the room seemed to spin and everything went black.

*

People were grabbing me and manhandling me and I was dumped in the chair. I opened my eyes to find two strangers staring at me. The first was a very large black woman in a blue nurse's uniform. I wondered about the system of colour coding in the hospital – was having stripes senior to solid blue? Maybe like sergeant's stripes in the army? Her beefy arms were crossed over her extremely ample chest and I wondered how she managed it and decided she must have exceptionally long arms. Her expression combined an unfriendly frown with deep suspicion.

'What you doin' here? Who are you?' The man standing next to her put a hand on her arm.

'If you could let me ask the questions please, Sister?' She glared at him and muttered something under her breath but reluctantly took a symbolic step backwards. He bent down and looked me in the eyes. He was in his fifties, slim, and his suit was worn but well cut. Intelligent blue eyes under recently barbered receding salt and pepper hair regarded me speculatively.

'We found you lying on the floor here, next to the bed. As the lady said, kindly tell us who you are and what you're doing here.'

It all came flooding back and I craned my neck to peer around him. It hadn't been some kind of dream or hallucination. There she was. Nicky. None of it made sense and it was only when I felt his hand shaking my shoulder that I tore my gaze away.

'Are you alright? Do you need a doctor?' He took his hand away when he saw that my attention had returned.

'Your name? And why you're here?' I made an effort to bring myself under control and focus on what he was saying.

'I'm sorry, it's just … my name is Mark Crawford. I'm here because … er … ' I stopped as I realised what it was going to sound like. *I had a hangover, you see, and then I just had this compulsion, like a voice in my head and it brought me here.* I grabbed his arm.

'Why is she here? What's wrong, what happened to her? Has she been in an accident?' He turned to the sister.

'Would you mind, Sister? Let me talk to him alone for a while.' She rolled her eyes and left. He pulled up the other visitor's chair until we were face to face, our knees almost touching. It felt intimidating and I leaned back so that he wasn't quite as much in my face. He looked at me steadily.

'You know her?' I nodded.

'Yes, she's Nicky – Nicola – Russell. At least she used to be. She might have married since then.' He raised his eyebrows.

'So you haven't seen her for some time?'

'Ten years,' I said, and drifted away for a moment.

Ten years. Bloody hell. Ten bloody years since she dumped me and ripped out my heart and jumped on it and did the fandango on it. In high heels. Ten aimless years of booze and a string of one night stands hardly any of which I could remember in any detail. Nights – when I could remember them at all - that merged into an amorphous memory of anonymous sweaty thrashing about seeking release and then just wanting them to leave as quickly as possible so that I didn't have to pretend it meant anything or that I wanted to see them again or to have to try and remember their names.

'What's wrong with you? Are you on drugs?

Medication? Are you sure you don't need a doctor?' He looked taken aback when I laughed.

'There's nothing wrong with me that a full English breakfast or a Bloody Mary wouldn't cure,' I said. 'I'm sorry. I just have a hell of a hangover and now this ... ' I gestured at the bed and once I had looked again couldn't tear myself away.

'So if you hadn't seen her for ten years, what are you doing here? How did you know she was here in the first place?'

All at once I felt very tired. I looked him in the eye.

'I'll tell you exactly why I'm here. And you won't believe a word I'm saying. But even so you're going to tell me why she's here and what happened to her. Deal?' He permitted himself a faint smile.

'Try me. Deal.'

So I did. I told him everything, step by step, blow by blow until I passed out and they found me. As I was finishing a thought struck me. I really wasn't firing on all cylinders or I would have asked earlier.

'That's everything exactly as it happened. Who are you, by the way? Why are you asking me all these questions?'

'I'm with the police, Mr Crawford. My name is Evans, Detective Inspector Evans. As to Miss Russell, that's a long story. But right now she has bruising on the face and arms and is suffering from some sort of concussion. She was admitted last night, unconscious, and has remained so. As far as the hospital is concerned she's stable and there is no sign of other injuries. She has had a scan and they can't see any damage to the brain or cranium and what it amounts to is that they are just waiting for her to wake up.

There are signs of old fractures to the ribs and legs, but they are healed and not current.'

'But what actually happened?' I asked. 'Was she in a car accident? Mugged? What? Tell me!' He gave me an odd, considering look and seemed to come to a decision.

'I've been up most of the night and could use a cup of coffee, and by the look of it so could you. There's a place across the road. We can talk there.' He saw my reluctance to leave and put a hand on my arm.

'Don't worry, we won't be long, and she'll still be here when we get back. Come on. Let's go.'

The place across the road was a small Italian café and the double espresso was strong and rich and made me feel more human. The throbbing was receding by the minute and I wolfed down a ham and cheese sandwich while Evans talked.

'You told me I wouldn't believe your story, and in the normal course of events I certainly wouldn't have. But when you hear what I know you will understand why I didn't dismiss it out of hand. I take it from the way you looked at her that you were close back then? In love?' I nodded and he continued.

'Do you know anything about what happened to her after the two of you split up?' I shrugged. The memory was still very painful and I sometimes found it difficult to believe any of it had really happened.

'Not really. I heard she had moved to New York to try and get a modelling career going, but that was the last I heard. I travelled around quite a bit soon after that and when I came back to London I had lost touch with most of our mutual friends. So that was pretty much that. Strange, isn't it, how it happens.' He nodded sympathetically and I was already warming to him. I'm like that. I tend to make snap judgements about people, and have never had reason to reverse my initial opinion. Evans seemed very genuine and I trusted him instinctively.

'Well, I first met Miss Russell about a year ago. We'd had a report of a domestic disturbance. Normally I wouldn't get involved in something like that, but we were very short-handed that night – there was a protest march that got out of hand – and I happened to be only a couple of minutes away so I said I'd handle it. It was a flat near Oxford Circus and there was no answer when I tried the intercom, so I kept buzzing different flats until somebody let me in.' He paused.

'Why do people do that? When they haven't got a clue who it is? It's a mystery. Anyway. I went up to the first floor to the flat number I'd been given and knocked on the door. At first there was no response, but I kept banging on the door, saying it was the police and that I wasn't going to leave until they opened up. When the door eventually opened it was a big man, muscular, black hair, odd accent, American and something else, French maybe. What really gave me the creeps was that he seemed to have no expression at all, no curiosity, no fear of the police, no bluster, no pompous fake outrage, all the things I've seen a million times in my career. He asked what I wanted, I said there had been a report of a domestic disturbance, and he said he didn't know what I was talking about. I asked if there was anybody else in the flat and he hesitated a fraction of a second too long and I just pushed past him.'

'Miss Russell was on the floor and she wasn't

moving. I could see one arm was at an unnatural angle and called for more police and an ambulance. I had him arrested on suspicion of assault and went to the hospital with her. A dislocated arm and a punch to the jaw, which is what had knocked her out.'

I was hanging on his every word, the remains of my sandwich forgotten on the plate. I could feel a rising tide of fury inside me, but reminded myself that what he was describing was a year ago and controlled it as best I could.

'When I spoke to her the next day and asked her what had happened she looked terrified and refused to press charges. I tried to persuade her to let me get her belongings and find her somewhere safe to be away from the man, but she refused. I got quite angry, as I recall. It's the frustration, you see. I know types like him. They promise to change and sometimes manage to control themselves for a time but in the end they are brutes and the brute overcomes the veneer of conventional behaviour and fear of consequences and they lash out. And take pleasure from it. I said all that to her, but she was adamant.

'I couldn't change her mind but insisted on accompanying her. Since we couldn't charge him he had been released and was waiting at the flat. He was all over her, solicitous and apologising and fussing. It made me sick. She went to lie down and I took him to one side. His name was Bruno, by the way. Bruno Maudire. Mean anything to you?' I shook my head.

'Anyway, I was as unpleasant and menacing as I could be, and told him that if there was any recurrence I would make it my personal mission to make the rest of his life hell in addition to the legal consequences which I would make sure were pursued to the utmost. But I could see it was water off a duck's back. And then last night one of my colleagues picked up a report of an assault with the woman victim taken to hospital unconscious and remembered her name because I had unloaded my frustration to him over a drink after the episode a year ago. I popped in to have a look at her and went for a coffee. When I came back a little later the nurse and I found you on the floor. The rest you know.'

I ran through everything he had told me but something still puzzled me and I shook my head slowly.

'All that explains why she is here, but not why she went back to this Bruno character or why you implied you might believe what I told you. There's more, isn't there. Tell me everything. Please.' He nodded reluctantly.

'You're right. After I gave up my attempts to stop her going back that day a year ago, we started to talk, and we seemed to get on and found it came very easily. It doesn't happen very often.'

'No, it doesn't,' I said. 'I had the same feeling the minute we started talking.' He raised his eyebrows and smiled a tired smile.

'That's a very un-British thing to say, but thank you. But that's not the point. I was trying to understand what she saw in a brute like him when she said something very strange. *He has shown me things I never knew existed,* that's what she said and when she saw my face she laughed. *No, not sex, silly! He can take me places in his mind, and sometimes he can get into mine, it's hard to explain, he has this strange ability* ... she saw my expression and changed the subject. And hearing something similar from you now ... well, I felt I should give you the benefit of the doubt, at least. Can you shed any light on any of this?' I shook my head, my mind in turmoil. I still had the feeling he was holding something back but didn't want to antagonise him, and got to my feet.

'I want to go back to her.' He stood up too, and I threw some money on the table when another thought struck me.

'What about this man, this Bruno? What have you done about him?' He sighed and we crossed the road.

'I sent a couple of men to the flat but there was nobody there. She was found with her bag with her keys and ID and they went in and he's gone, no men's clothes, shoes, shaving kit, no trace of him. Just her stuff. So I'm having his details circulated, and asked the neighbours to let us know if they saw him, but there's really not much else I can do.'

We arrived back in room 327 and nothing at all had changed. Evans excused himself saying he had some things to attend to, and I gave him my mobile number and he shut the door softly behind him. I pulled up a chair close to the bed and took her hand in both of mine.

'It's me, Nicky,' I whispered. 'It's Mark. I'm here. I'll stay with you. Please wake up, Nicky. Please,' I lowered my lips and kissed her palm and even with all the hospital odours the warm smell of her was shockingly familiar. It was like a physical jolt and a wave of tiredness engulfed me. The hangover – what the hell *had* I done last night? - and the emotional roller coaster of seeing Nicky again and Evan's bizarre story all seemed to hit me at once. The room was dimly lit, the air conditioning was a quiet, soothing murmur in the background, and I laid my head on the cool, crisp sheets with her hand against my cheek and closed my eyes.

*

My rest didn't last very long. Something very hot was burning me and I squirmed uncomfortably and opened my eyes and shut them again very quickly. There was a searingly bright sun overhead and I became aware that I was lying on hard, stony ground with jagged pebbles digging uncomfortably into my back. I sat up and there was Nicky, holding my hands and grinning from ear to ear. She looked awful. Her head was still wrapped in bandages and she was wearing the dark blue hospital gown she had been lying in and still had the shiner but her blue eyes were sparkling as she leaned forward and hugged me so tightly I had to eventually push her away to breathe.

'You found me! Oh, Marky, you found me! I somehow knew you would!' *Marky*. I had always had a love / hate relationship with that. I hated the infantile way it sounded but only she had ever called me that and that made it special and somehow okay. I had so many questions I didn't know where to start and found myself spluttering incoherently.

'Nicky! What … how … where the hell are we? How did we get here? We were in the hospital … ' my words faded away and we just sat there looking at each other. She jumped to her feet and took my hand again.

'Come on! Let's get out of the sun or you're going to burn up! You always burned so easily!' I let her pull me up and really looked around for the first time. We were on a slope at the foot of an enormous cliff of red sandstone that made my neck hurt as I leaned backwards to look at the top far above us. An endless plain of ochres and reds and umbers and yellows stretched to the horizon where it met a line of weirdly shaped crags like distant, misshapen sentinels.

She was pulling me towards the cliff face and I couldn't for the life of me think where she thought there might be shade – I couldn't see any anywhere.

'God, I wish there was a cave or an overhang or something,' I said. I could feel my skin heating up and knew that very soon it would burn enough to cause me real discomfort, and not for the first time cursed my North European colouring of sandy hair, blue eyes and pale, freckled skin. She was jumping up and down with glee the way I remembered her doing when she was about to give me a present or spring a surprise on me and I blinked in disbelief as a cave mouth appeared before us, the interior promising shade and coolness.

I knew it had not been there a second ago. I had been looking at that very place and we were only ten or fifteen feet away. I let myself be pulled inside and escaping the furnace outside and feeling the cool stone under my hand felt wonderful. But I was also starting to feel increasingly disoriented by what was happening and sat down abruptly. I took her hands and pulled her down beside me and made a huge effort not to lose it completely. I spoke slowly and carefully.

'Nicky. Please. Explain to me exactly what is going on. Where we are. How we got here. Now, before you say anything else. *Tell me!*' I shouted the last words and she pulled away, pouting.

'Ten years and that's all you have to say to me?' I must have looked dangerously close to violence because she put her hand to my cheek.

'I'm sorry. I'd forgotten how easy it was to get you going. I'm truly sorry.' She stared out of the cave mouth into the shimmering heat haze beyond.

'This is going to be very hard, Marky. You're just going to have to take my word for all of it. Please try and keep an open mind. Will you do that?' I nodded and she took a deep breath.

'This isn't real, Mark. I made this place up, everything you see, created it and built it up bit by bit in my mind. I'd always wanted to go to Arizona and Death Valley and the Grand Canyon, all those monumental places with those weird shapes and fantastic colours. Maybe because all of it is done by nature, not by us, I don't know, but it always fascinated me. So when I came to make a place to escape to I suppose that's where I got it from, all the things I had seen in films and documentaries and magazines. It's all stored away somewhere in your brain, you know. Everything you've ever seen and experienced, it's all there if you know how to get at it.'

She paused and seemed to fade for a moment, closing her eyes.

'And Bruno showed you how, did he?' I said. The bitterness in my voice made her shrink into herself and she took my face in both her hands and looked earnestly into my eyes.

'How do you know about Bruno? I bet it was Evans, wasn't it. I liked him, such a nice man. But it doesn't really matter. Listen to me. I am so sorry about what happened between us back then,' she said softly. 'I couldn't be more sorry and have been sorry ever since. But please, please put that aside for now. You need to understand.'

I was tired of the whole thing. I didn't understand any of it and wondered if I was going mad or had inadvertently taken some drug like LSD. And then I had a flash of illumination. Of course! Why on earth hadn't I realised it straight away! This was all a dream – what else could it be? All the weird and inexplicable things – that's exactly what happens in dreams. I let out a long sigh as the tension drained out of me and relaxed. I might as well go along for the ride – after all, what choice did I have until I woke up? It was certainly very different from any other dream I'd ever had.

'Go on,' I said. 'You have my undivided attention. If this isn't real, what am I doing here? This rock I'm sitting on seems pretty damn hard and real!' She smiled a wan, tired smile.

'I made this place to escape him,' she said. 'And yes, he did show me how although he didn't know he was doing it. Oh Mark. You've no idea what it was like.' I held out my arms and she snuggled up to me and feeling her so close to me took my breath away.

'I met him after I'd been in New York for a while,' she continued. 'He was Vice-President or something like that for a big ad agency and saw me in their office and asked me out. I had kept myself to myself and when all the agents and photographers and producers realised I wasn't going to let them into my pants I ended up with very few friends. He was totally different from anyone I had ever met – he had this animal magnetism and this Cajun accent that seemed very exotic to me. I found myself drawn to him and somehow couldn't stop myself. So we went out and I moved in with him a week later.'

She must have felt the way my body stiffened at

the thought of her living with this creep. I reminded myself of how many women I had slept with in the last ten years and forced myself put the images of her in bed with him to one side before they made me crazy. She must have sensed I had my anger under control and went on.

'For quite a while it was fun. Lots of drinks and parties and expensive dinners and I even got a few modelling jobs and time passed and it all seemed to be going so well. There were times when he seemed like a total stranger but whenever I had thoughts like that it was if something just made them go away. But then he asked me to marry him and that forced me to really look at what I was doing and I had to face the fact that I didn't love him. I've never really loved anybody but you, Marky. Never. No matter what you think, that's the truth.'

'Anyway. When he saw I wasn't going to marry him and might even leave, he told me he had a secret he had never revealed to anyone else, that it would change my life, and that he was willing to share it with me if I would stay with him. I hadn't actually decided to leave him anyway, so I agreed. Oh Mark.'

'He was able to do … this.' She encompassed everything we could see with a sweep of her hand.

'Somehow he could make these constructed worlds in his mind and after trying for some time he found he could draw me into them too. You can't imagine what it was like. He could make it be anywhere. We could stand on top of Everest or in the middle of a rain forest or on a beach in Hawaii or walk on Broadway or explore the Vatican … and it would be just us, an empty construct like a fairy playground to explore and do stupid things in. A lot of time went by before the novelty wore off and I started to see what he was doing. He was making me addicted to the thrill of coming home to a New York apartment and minutes later wandering through St Paul's or Buckingham Palace. It was utterly fantastic and hugely exciting. Like a drug.'

'But then he started doing things that seemed daring and harmless at first but over time forced me to realise what an unstable and fundamentally destructive person he was. I think he tried to hold back his true nature as long as he could and then one day he just couldn't any more.'

'I remember it was in the Metropolitan Museum in New York and I was revelling in having the place to ourselves and looking at the exhibits when he went up to this really ancient statue – Sumerian, I think - and looked at me with this grin that gave me the shivers and just pushed the statue over and it smashed into little pieces. I mean it was irreplaceable and by some miracle had survived thousands of years and you should have seen how his face lit up.'

'He was like boy who has finally remembered how to pull the wings off flies and from then on there was no holding him back. It sickened me and the very next day I told him I was leaving. He laughed and didn't believe me until I was at the door and that was the first time he beat me up. He was so angry he lost control completely and I can still hear what he said. Normally he had sounded like anybody else, but when he was really angry he reverted to this thick Cajun accent.'

"You think you can leave me, *coo-yôn* woman? I put a spell on you, *dôn matta* what you do, I find you and I hurt you bad! *To konprann?*"

'It was awful and I finally realised that there was something he had done, some way he had of controlling me and that the thing he shared with me was the sugar coating on the pill, the distraction and demonstration that he could do things nobody else could. I never found out what it was – some kind of voodoo or whatever, I just don't know. They have an awful lot of strange things where he came from, but he would never tell me.'

'I suppose I still couldn't really admit to myself that I couldn't be free any more. The next time I thought I had planned it carefully and ran away to another model's apartment while he was out. He found me in a couple of hours and that time it was worse.'

'I sort of lost the will to try after that. And then he would refuse to "take" me with him to punish me and I missed the adrenaline rush so much I would beg him to forgive me. How he loved that. And how I hated myself for being so weak.'

'Then one day I was looking at a magazine and it was a beautiful beach somewhere and I was daydreaming what it would be like and then I was there, doing just what he was able to do. But it wasn't complete, it had all kinds of fuzzy bits where I hadn't paid attention and so I practised and practised and was able to have my quiet time when he wasn't there and go to the places I wanted to go.'

'We moved to London a little over a year ago when the agency asked him to take over their offices here. By this time he was in a descending spiral and started experimenting with more and more horrible things, you wouldn't believe. Looking at photos of battles and murders and atrocities and taking us there and recreating all the dead bodies and gore to gloat over like a ghoul. It was awful, just awful. And he was beating me more and more often.'

I was stunned. This was one very weird dream and seemed to be going on for a hell of a long time, but I thought I had spotted an inconsistency.

'It was only ever the two of you, isn't that what you said? How did he get the bodies … ' I snapped my fingers and answered my own question.

'Of course, they were dead, inanimate and so he could recreate them. I think I get it. Insofar as I get any of this. Maybe I don't. What happened to you this time?' She held me tighter.

'From what happened before and things he would let slip from time to time I came to believe that this spell or whatever he had done to me meant he could sense me like a bloodhound, some of kind of connection he could home in on. He would find me so quickly when I ran away because once he had managed to include me in … these things he did, it strengthened that bond. It's hard to explain. So this time I thought I would be clever and not only escape him physically but also using his own abilities that he didn't know I had acquired.'

'I practised and kept working on it and made this place and I packed a bag and was heading for a women's refuge where I was going to ask to stay and hope he wouldn't be able to find me and then come here until he gave up. And hoped they could protect me if he did find me. But he came back early and found me on the street and he hit me really hard and I think I must have knocked my head on something because I found myself here. And when I saw the way I was dressed I realised I must be in hospital.'

I felt an increasing sense of unease as she spoke. This was feeling less and less like a dream. They didn't have these detailed narratives, somebody speaking at length. But my rational mind told me it simply *couldn't* be real and I surrendered to its internal logic while it lasted.

'Tell me quickly! Can I get back? Leave here? And if I can, will I be able to come back?' She nodded but clutched my hand.

'Yes, you can, but please stay, Mark, don't leave me alone!'

'I'll be back, don't worry! But tell me how, come on there's no time!' She sighed and sagged back against the cave wall. She looked worn out.

'Just close your eyes and will yourself back. And then touch me and wish yourself back here.' I kissed her and closed my eyes, imagining the hospital room. I opened them and I was by the bed and she was lying there unmoving exactly as she had been. The door opened and Evans came in. He must have seen the wild look in my eyes because he stopped dead in his tracks.

'Mr Crawford! What's wrong! Has something happened?' I had to control my sense of urgency and try and be coherent.

'He hit her and she must have knocked her head on the pavement. I think she's in real danger – the man's a total nutter and weirdo. Put an armed guard on her and don't leave her alone. Please!' He stared at me.

'We know he hit her. A couple of witnesses came forward – he ran off when they approached and shouted at him. Do you think he'll come here? How do you know?' I stood in front of him and gripped his arm.

'I know that you know there's something very weird going on here, and now I know it too. Please! Promise me you'll have her guarded. Oh, and if I seem to be asleep and holding on to her on no account disturb me – that's really important!' I let go of him, sat down and rested my head on the bed and held her hands and willed myself back to … to whatever that place was.

She seemed to have been dozing and threw her arms around me and hugged me and gave me a kiss.

'Marky! You're back! I'm so glad.' She looked very, very tired and I made her sit down next to me.

'What was your plan?' I asked urgently. 'Were you just going to sit here forever?' She got that small-girl look that had sometimes made my heart melt and at other times had irritated the hell out of me.

'I didn't have a plan beyond this,' she whispered. 'All I could think about was to get away … '

My attention was caught by a movement on the plain below. It was far away, but the primitive parts of our brains are still very attuned to pick up the slightest movement. I pointed and she gasped.

'No, that can't be – we should be the only living things here – that's the way it always worked!' I had a sinking feeling in the pit of my stomach. Then I remembered how effortlessly she had made the cave.

'Make a pile of rocks to hide the cave mouth!' She nodded and there it was, instantly, a mound of boulders and debris in front of the entrance. She sagged against the side of the cave.

I didn't know how long it would take Evans to get a guard on her in the hospital, or even if he would do it at all based on my manic outburst. I crawled out and peered carefully around the edge of the rock wall. To my dismay the distant figure had veered to a course aiming directly towards us and I knew it was him. I don't know how, but I just knew and I felt an unmanning sense of panic because I didn't have any idea what to do.

'Nicky, we have to leave here! It's him and he's heading straight for us!' Her eyes widened in panic.

'No! It can't be! It's impossible! Unless ... '

'Unless what!' I yelled. She seemed to shrink into herself.

'Maybe there are things he didn't tell me,' she whispered. I rolled my eyes and risked another peek and now the figure was close enough to discern the shape of a man striding purposefully towards us. I grabbed Nicky.

'We need to run! Make a tunnel to the back of the mountain! Come on!' I pulled her to her feet and headed for the blank wall of rock at the back of the cave. I looked at her impatiently and my heart lurched as I saw that she seemed to be running out of steam. She was looking very pale and holding on to me to support herself.

'Nicky! Please try! Imagine a tunnel opening up in front of us!' And miraculously, there it was. As we stumbled along rather than ran I had another idea.

'Close up the tunnel behind us, Nicky. Imagine it becoming solid rock again after us.' She nodded and we were plunged into a stygian darkness. Shit! I hadn't thought of that but then Nicky made the tunnel straight as a ruler and it expanded to three or four times its previous size and we saw a dot of light up ahead. We ran and ran and it became bigger. By the time we staggered out into the sunlight she was exhausted and I was half carrying her.

I made her seal the mountain behind us and we collapsed and lay on our backs, catching our breath. Nicky was sobbing with fear and exhaustion.

'Oh Mark. I don't how he can be here. He's going to kill us, I know it. Oh God, I'm sorry I got you into this. I'm sorry.' My brain was working furiously but not coming up with anything remotely useful.

'Quick! Tell me more about how this place works! Can you imagine anything into existence? A weapon? Anything like that? Nicky! Snap out of it and help me!' She shook her bandaged head to clear it and when she spoke her voice was tired and hesitant.

'As far as I know once you've created the world you can manipulate some things in it, like I just did. But you can't make things appear that weren't in your original creation. Oh and you always bring with you the stuff that's on you like clothes and stuff.' She plucked at the blue hospital gown.

The base of the other side of the mountain where we had emerged was mercifully still in shadow, but the shaded strip was narrowing. I made Nicky think an overhanging ledge into existence and helped her scramble up the slope to it. We lay flat in deep shadow and moments later I saw Bruno's powerful figure appear around the far edge of the mountain. He was wearing combat fatigues and had something in his hand that looked like a long knife or machete and was idly swinging it to and fro.

'Nicola! Where are you! You know I'm going to find you, I always do! Come out now, my *beb*, and we'll let bygones be bygones, what you say? *Dôn* be so *coo-yôn!* Come on, you know you want to!' He sounded as if he was talking to a naughty child, his voice wheedling and full of false bonhomie.

To my horror Nicky was shaking her head and trying to get to her feet. I had no time to think and pulled her down and hit her on the chin as hard as I dared and her head snapped back and her eyes rolled up and I caught her and lowered her onto the ledge. I saw him falter and guessed he must have lost his signal or whatever the hell it was. I had to clap a hand over my mouth to stifle an hysterical giggle at the absurdity of the whole situation.

Was this dream never going to end? I decided to see if I could do what Nicky did and concentrated on a ridge of pale stone a good six or seven hundred metres on the man's other side, away from us. I imagined dislodging some small stones from the ridge and letting them tumble down. Nothing happened. Shit. This was a dream, for God's sake. I ought to be able to do weird stuff here as well. I felt ridiculously and unreasonably aggrieved. Bruno started a wide circuit that fortunately didn't bring him close to us and I took my chance and imagined myself back in the hospital.

Evans was sitting by the bed and started as I dropped Nicky's hand and leaped to my feet.

'Quick! I need a weapon and I need it right now! Do you have a gun?' He shook his head.

'Sorry, I have an armed guard on the way but you have no idea what that cost me in favours or what could happen to me if this goes pear-shaped. Why … '

'How long before he gets here?' I gasped. He looked at his watch.

'Any time in the next half an hour,' he began and I exploded in frustration.

'He's in there! Bruno! Somehow he's in there and he's looking for her! I need a fucking weapon, and I need it right now!' He looked at me and at Nicky's comatose form and nodded.

'Wait here,' he said, 'I'll be as quick as I can.' I was dancing from one foot to the other with impatience when he came back and handed me some objects.

'God help me, I must be crazy. This is all I could find. That's a scalpel, be careful or you could have a finger off. A couple of syringes. And this. I found it in the storeroom. It's part of a disassembled bed but it's pretty solid.' It was a hollow tube of heavy steel about a metre long and it felt good in my hand.

'Thank you! Listen, one last thing. As soon as the gun arrives put it in my hand with the safety off. Will you do that? Please?' He stared at me.

'How the hell am I going to do that? It's impossible! I can't just … '

'Find a way! I'm counting on you!' I sat down in what I had come to think of as my "taking off" position holding her hand and thought myself back.

Nicky was groaning and rubbing her chin. I saw Bruno in the distance stamping about randomly and now he was angry.

'Nicola! Don't try and be *canaille!* Come out this instant or it will be the worse for you, girl!' He stopped in his tracks and stood absolutely still. Slowly his head turned towards us and we shrank back into the shadow of the ledge. He started walking unhurriedly in our direction. I was suddenly struck by an idea that was so blindingly obvious I couldn't believe I hadn't thought of it straight away.

'Nicky! Why can't you just think yourself back to the hospital and we can both just get out of here like

I've been doing!' She was still groggy and even rubbing her jaw seemed to take all her concentration. She shook her head despondently.

'I can't, Mark. I came here while I was still barely conscious and now I'm still unconscious over there in the real world. Unless I wake up I'm stuck here.' Her eyes fluttered but widened when she saw that Bruno was now much closer.

'Shit. I know! Break off a big boulder and dump it on him! Come on!' I looked at her and to my horror she had collapsed and was as out of it here as she was back in the hospital. I really, really didn't like the way this dream was going and squeezed my eyes shut and willed myself to wake up. Nothing happened. Bruno was now standing at the foot of the outcrop below the ledge where we were, and looking up at me with a puzzled frown.

'Who the hell are you? So the found herself a *peeshwank podna,* eh? Too bad for you, my fren'. She my toy so if you got any prayers you better damn well say them.'

He started clambering up the rocky slope towards us, never taking his dark eyes off me. He had thick, black eyebrows and a cropped black bush of hair and looked mad and dangerous. *Very* dangerous. I wasted a second or two lost in incredulity that Nicky could possibly have been attracted to this man.

By now his eyes were level with the ledge and they lit up when he saw her inert form.

'There you are, *beb,* not long now and you will be with me where you belong. I just have to swat this *p'tit boug* first.'

He was swinging the machete and bared his teeth at me in a humourless grin. Dream or no dream, I was really frightened now. More like scared shitless. My legs were trembling and I felt frozen with terror and it was only when his eyes rested on Nicky and became greedy with anticipation that I snapped out of it. I had the steel rod in one hand, hidden behind my leg and the scalpel in the other. He saw it and threw back his head and roared with laughter.

'Oh, that's funny. *Qui c'est q'ca?* What a mighty weapon! Is your dick that small too?' At that moment all reason left me. The whole situation was so utterly devoid of reason that I suppose it wasn't that great a leap.

While he was still laughing and shaking his head I launched myself at him. I rather agreed with him about the scalpel so I dropped it and swung at him with all my strength. He shouted something incoherent in surprise and there was a loud clang as he instinctively brought up the machete to ward me off. It skidded down the bar and I felt a searing pain as it sliced a glancing blow across my forearm. The momentum pushed him against the side of the cliff and me in the opposite direction and I fell down the side of the outcrop.

The metal bar flew from my fingers and some still-functioning part of my mind knew that its distant clatter meant it was far out of reach. Sharp stones tore at my arms and side and I landed heavily on my back and hit my head with a sickening thud and lay sprawled at the base of the outcrop where he had been standing only minutes earlier. My vision blurred and my chest heaved and I seemed to hurt all over. It was as if I was wearing a garment that produced pain and I had this hallucinatory vision of a suited and softly spoken tailor in a gentlemen's outfitters standing back and saying, *so you see sir this model is particularly effective at distributing even amounts of pain ...*

I giggled at the absurdity of it but a renewed wave of pain made me groan and my sight came into focus again and Bruno was standing by the ledge rubbing his shoulder and grimacing. But he was still holding the machete and didn't seem badly hurt at all. He looked down on me and shook his head.

'You surprise me, *chudut,* whoever you are. I did not think you had it in you! But it is time to end this. You die now.' He came down towards me, watching his step on the loose stones but also watching me with a little more respect than he had shown earlier. I looked around desperately but couldn't see my metal rod or a stone bigger than a walnut or anything at all I could use to defend myself. My right arm had a gash a couple of inches long and vivid red blood was dripping onto the dusty ground.

I closed my eyes and willed myself back to the hospital room. Evans was in the middle of an argument with a wiry, athletic looking policeman wearing a dark blue flak vest and a buttoned black holster. They both stopped and gawped at me and I saw a spatter of red droplets on the violet floor and had a flash of what I must have looked like. Without hesitation I leaped at the man with the gun and hit him on the chin as hard as I could. White-hot pain shot up my arm and I thought I might have broken a finger or two but he dropped like a marionette whose wires had been cut.

Evans caught him and eased his fall and I scrabbled at the catch on the holster and pulled out a heavy black automatic. I knew nothing about guns and thrust it at Evans.

'Take off the safety! Life or death! No time!' He flicked a small slide and handed it back to me without question and I have never been so grateful to anybody in my entire life. I grabbed Nicky's hand and thought myself back to the other place and Bruno was standing over me with the machete raised and I gripped the pistol with both hands and squeezed the trigger again and again until all I could hear was a metallic clicking.

Bruno was wearing a light brown tee shirt and red spots bloomed all over it and then he was gone. I dropped the gun and painfully levered myself onto my elbow and he was lying motionless in the dust, a widening pool of blood seeping out from under him and glistening darkly in the harsh sunlight. I thought myself back to the hospital room, remembering at the last minute to pick up the gun. I slumped to the floor and the policeman I had cold-cocked snatched it up and pointed it at me, face red with fury.

I looked at my arm and it was still bleeding and I was starting to feel light-headed, and not just from the blood loss. The enormity and strangeness of everything that had happened since I woke up that morning and the feeling of being in a nightmare from which there was no escape all came crashing down at me.

'Go ahead,' I said and laughed and even I could hear the edge of hysteria in my voice.

'You go right ahead. Go on, you know you want to.' His face became even more suffused and Evans quickly stepped between us.

'Put the gun down, Constable,' he said. The man was still trying to point it at me and he grasped it firmly by the barrel.

'Let it go now or I'll see you never carry a firearm again,' he said and the steely conviction in his voice finally got through. The constable's colour and breathing started to return to normal and Evans expertly ejected the magazine.

'Care to explain this Constable?' he said. The man looked confused and inspected the magazine, pushing at the spring mechanism with a finger in bewilderment.

'It's empty, sir!' he said. 'But it can't be! I checked the load myself before leaving! How … who could … ' he ran dry and stared at Evans. My head was swimming and I didn't feel too good. I cleared my throat.

'Er … bleeding to death here? Need a doctor?' I said and my voice was faint and trembling like an old man's.

*

In the end Evans convinced the constable to tell his mate in the armoury he had somehow lost the magazine and to persuade him to fudge the records. The doctor who fixed me up was appalled that this had happened in the hospital, but Evans was after all a Detective Inspector so the question of reporting it to the police was happily avoided. I spent a few hours in another room sleeping off the pain killers they gave me and was awake when Evans looked in on me later that night.

He asked how I was feeling. My arm throbbed like hell and I felt as if I had been run over by a bus and told him so. He sat in a chair and stretched out his long legs with a sigh and for a few moments we were silent, lost in our thoughts.

'Why did you do it?' I finally said. 'Even if you're the most open minded and sympathetic character in the world, nobody would have done what you did. Nobody. Yet you believed me and helped me and even gave me weapons without question. I don't understand. Why?' He smiled and shrugged.

'When I first came to see her before you arrived, I took her hand. And just for a moment, literally for a couple of seconds, I was standing beside her in a bloody great desert and she was still in her hospital clothes and bandages and we just looked at each other. And then I was back here. And then you started babbling about her being there and that's how I knew you were telling the truth. So tell me what happened.'

When I had finished he shrugged again.

'Good riddance,' was all he said. I was feeling much stronger and got off the bed and we walked down the corridor together to room 327.

Nicky still lay there motionless. I looked at Evans and he nodded and I took her hand. She was sitting on the ledge where I had left her, watching the sunset she had created and I have to say it was spectacularly beautiful. I looked down and Bruno's body was gone and I raised my eyebrows.

'I got rid of him,' was all she would say.

*

My life is very different now, and I go to visit Nicky in the hospital most days. They say she could still wake up at any time, or never. They just don't know. I usually take something nice, maybe champagne or a picnic lunch and we sit on the veranda of the house she has made — with some design ideas of mine that I am rather pleased with - or look at the fabulous canopy of stars if she chooses for it to be night time.

I see her clearly now, her limitations, her weaknesses and her inability to foresee the consequences of her actions. The anger has long since disappeared and with it the love I once felt all those years ago. It has become more like an easy friendship under very weird circumstances and we don't feel the need to talk much about what went before.

I hardly drink at all these days except when I'm with her, or when I meet up with Evans. He too has become a good friend and it's good to have someone who knows what really happened. I've asked him to try and join us sometimes but he just smiles and shakes his head.

Soulmates

Some things have to be believed to be seen.

Ralph Hodgson

Ahuv was having a bad day. Strictly speaking, angels (for that is what he was) didn't have days at all, eternity being more or less what the word suggests. But he found it convenient to choose a world and use its natural cycles to introduce divisions into his labours. And let's face it, he thought, I don't eat, I don't sleep, I just am and time just is and my little corner of the universe just is. If I didn't have something out there that changed predictably it would get much more difficult just to keep track of things.

Like any job he had his slack periods and spent a lot of time – really, really a *lot* of time – thinking about the nature of his never-ending task. He was full of admiration for his boss – who wouldn't be? – but some things really made him wonder. His own job for instance. There were times when the scope of it really staggered him. Okay, he had been given the tools to do the job, he couldn't deny that.

His gaze fell on the cluster. That was his personal name for it, the cluster. Like his boss it existed without a name and he, Ahuv (and here he tried to suppress a guilty flush of pride) was one of the very few entities that even knew it existed. Apart from the boss, of course. It floated in the middle of the infinite white space that was his workplace, his home ... basically his place. That's how he thought of it. My place.

It looked like a majestic cloud of fireflies, floating lazily and moving infinitesimally slowly, fading in and out of focus as it waited for him to use it. Even after all this time it still mesmerised him, the way the individual points of light randomly segued from one gorgeous shade to another, blue to green to mauve to white in endless elusive transitions.

It wasn't just the sight of it that still thrilled him. It was what it represented. Each one was a world, but most importantly a world with life, a little segment of the infinite variety of life in its infinite combinations. And each one of those worlds had life-forms with a soul. Well, each one that showed on the cluster, anyway. There were of course innumerable other worlds with either no life at all or with life-forms too simple, too primitive, too near the beginning of their long ascent (if they ever made it, which most did not) to have souls. Life had to reach a certain point, a crucial cusp where a certain threshold of decision-making and awareness beyond the blind search for food and purely instinctive fight or flight responses were about to appear.

Then and only then came the moment, the magical moment, when they were suffused with the – for want of a better word – divine spark. Thankfully for Ahuv the boss had designed that to happen automatically. He shuddered to think of the workload if it didn't. No, it would be impossible. Well, obviously not actually *impossible* – nothing was impossible, in one sense – but he couldn't see how he could have managed, even in his special place with his special talents.

He somehow always knew when the universe required his attention, and allowed himself to glide sedately towards the cluster. He let his hands drift lovingly through the cloud of lights and they quickly solidified into unchanging colours ready for his ministrations. Something caught his eye and he stared disbelievingly. One of the sparks of light had changed to a bright glowing crimson. Now that was impossible. None of the worlds ever showed up in red. *Ever.* Even though he had never seen it happen before he instantly knew that red meant some catastrophe, some calamitous eventuality that was unforeseen and given the nature of the boss unforeseen was a little hard to credit.

He reached out and brushed the red dot and it immediately expanded and Ashriel appeared before him. His normally serene face was twisted into a worried frown and now Ahuv was *really* worried. In all his admittedly somewhat isolated eternity he had never seen a worried celestial being. Their minds met in instantaneous communication.

Ashriel! What has happened!

Disaster! Unheard of! Never happened before!

For God's sake! (Sorry) Explain what is going on this instant!

It's these humans! HE went and made them in his own image and gave them dominion over the animals and now they're out of control! They multiply and multiply and one by one they find ways to mitigate all the plagues and diseases and disasters that kept their numbers in check for so long - I have to admit, I am sometimes quite impressed by the ingenious things they come up with ...

Ashriel! Will you stop babbling and tell me what the problem is!

Sorry. I'm finding it a bit hard to get to grips with it myself ...

Ashriel!

Yes, yes. The thing is, we are running out of souls to reincarnate and it's getting pretty close to breaking point! What am I going to do? There were only so many allocated to this world and I suppose even ... well, forgive me, but even HE never thought they would take off like this. I'm at my wit's end.

All these years the wars and plagues and famines did a pretty good job of keeping things manageable ... but the last hundred years or so have been like nothing else before it and ... well, I have to confess, it was all ticking over nicely and I suppose I took my eye off the ball ...

Took your eye off the ball! Do you have any idea of what you've allowed to happen? Never mind. I don't believe this. I have to think. How much time do I have?

Ummm ... not very much, I'm afraid. I sort of only just noticed, really ... a day? An Earth day, that is. Maybe a little less?

Ahuv flapped his wings and Ashriel disappeared. He floated in his vast amorphous white domain and for the first time in his existence experienced a sort of panic. There was only one thing for it. He had never considered such a thing or imagined the necessity for it but ... yes. He had to. The boss had to tell him what to do.

He closed his eyes and let his mind broadcast his need. When he opened them Vretil was watching him carefully. He had never seen the archangelic keeper of the Treasury of Sacred Books before but as with all celestial beings he knew at once who he was. He was said to be wiser than the other archangels and was also called "The Scribe of the Knowledge of the Most High." Ahuv started pouring out his troubled thoughts and Vretil held out a hand to forestall him.

It goes without saying that HE knows everything. And my message to you is this. You must make this right in your own way.

What! Make it right in my own way? What does that mean? How ...

But Vretil had already disappeared.

*

Ahuv floated immobile while his mind whirled and turned this way and that and got absolutely nowhere. His gaze kept going back to the red spark that was getting threateningly redder and darker all the time. He went back to the cluster and touched a blue light and its resident celestial being sprang into view. Several worlds later he paused. The exchange after he explained what he needed was the same each time.

What? You want me to transfer souls to another unit? How? That's unprecedented – and in any case we don't know how a (local name) soul would do in a … human, that's what they're called, aren't they? Oh yes! They're the ones created in HIS image, aren't they, I've heard about them. Hmmmm. Let me think about it. I'll contact you. Yes, yes, soon, I promise.

Ahuv's wings were drooping by now. Not that he actually needed them. He wasn't a bird and he wasn't tied by the usual laws of physics and aerodynamics. But the sight of the big white feathers hanging listlessly below his feet depressed him even further. All he could do now was wait.

*

His disconsolate reverie was interrupted when Ashriel appeared, looking rather pleased with himself.

Well, we have all been communicating and exchanging ideas, and I think we have come up with a plan.

Ahuv heaved a sigh of relief and waited for Ashriel to continue.

As you know HE designed all living things from the ground up, as it were. Michael once suggested it was an extension of the idea of free will – you know, start it off simple, give it almost limitless potential and see what they make of it. I think he was just guessing, actually – I don't think the boss ever shares the fundamentals with anybody, do you?

And did you know that my humans are the only ones ever to have figured it out? To actually manage to get down to the basic building blocks? I think that might have been a bit of a surprise even for HIM!

Ahuv couldn't bear Ashriel's legendary propensity for going off at a tangent for another nanosecond.

Will you get to the point!

Sorry, yes, I was getting to that. Once we looked at it that way, all we had to do was compare the – the humans call it DNA, can you imagine giving something so miraculous an acronym? They'll be praying to G next … anyway.

It turns out there's a world with a race of beings that isn't too far off the humans – totally different kettle of fish, though. They call themselves the Slelani and they're slow and placid and all they do is eat and occasionally try to reproduce but the good news is their fertility is low and only some of them manage and even if they do they generally only have one young in a lifetime. It will be eons before they increase in numbers if they ever do and in fact they are quite possibly at the beginning of a decline. So Gebril – he's responsible for that world, by the way - has agreed to let me have half his allocation! Problem solved!

Ahuv couldn't help having a niggling feeling that it shouldn't be this easy, but couldn't think of any objections. Nor did he have an alternative suggestion. His eye caught the red glow of Earth that had by now darkened to a deep ruby.

Very well, very well, please proceed. And thank you all for helping to solve this unprecedented problem.

Ashriel nodded and disappeared, and in minutes the red was fading from Earth and it was returning to its usual cheerful pastel blue.

*

He was a beautiful baby and a delight to his

parents. Later on at school he wasn't interested in sports or any energetic boyish pursuits at all. But he was curious. Curious to a degree that nearly drove his parents mad with his unremitting questions about everything. But stressful and wearing as his upbringing was for them, it did have a silver lining – his academic results were staggeringly good.

At a parent teacher evening at his school his mother was proudly describing his achievements to another mother who rather than showing the polite (and possibly envious) interest one might expect began to look more and more puzzled.

'Look, this is really strange, but it's exactly the same with our son. Just as you described it. And yet his brother who is only a year older is perfectly normal. What an odd coincidence.'

A teacher who was listening went back to her study afterwards and sat at her desk pondering. She too had noticed that her current crop of ten year olds was very different. And yet it was not all of them. She tried to think of what either group might have in common and ran her eyes down the class list, idly putting a little star next to the extraordinarily bright ones. She never knew what made her look at the birthdates next to the names but all at once she thought she had noticed something. She almost dismissed the thought but because it was her nature she checked it nonetheless.

And there it was. No doubt about it. There was a definite dividing line. All the bright ones were born on or after the 24th of July ten years ago. And all the "normal" ones were born before. She sat back and wondered what she could do with this information. She couldn't think of anything.

*

Even though a lot of time had passed, thousands of years in Earth terms, every now and then Ahuv would still steal a quick glance at Earth in case that horrible red colour made a reappearance. But that long-ago crisis was settling into his more distant past now, just one more drop in a vast ocean of memories. Whenever this happened he would admonish himself to let it go, that it had been a one-off and in any case now they knew how to deal with it if – horror of horrors – it should ever recur.

Once again his comfortable, drowsy reverie was interrupted by Ashriel's unannounced appearance. Ahuv would never forget how worried he had looked all that time ago. But this time he looked positively overwrought and his heart sank. Ashriel wasted no time in communicating with him.

I'm sorry! I'm sorry! Who could have foreseen this! You must prepare yourself!

For what! What's happened! For God's sake (sorry) tell me!

I told you humans were different, didn't I. And it's not all my fault, Gebril only told me about the slowness and low reproductive rate and that all sounded good! He should have told me!

In the grip of the closest an angel can come to rage Ahuv spread his vast wings and drew himself up to his full, terrifying height.

ASHRIEL! Will you stop that infernal (sorry) babbling and tell me what's happened!

Yes, of course, sorry, sorry, it's just so unimaginable … I'm trying to tell you! You know how we talk about the divine spark … and you know we say that almost interchangeably with souls … well, it seems our understanding was the tiniest bit flawed …

Ahuv exerted all his not inconsiderable will power to remain calm and let Ashriel tell it in his own way as it seemed impossible to deflect him from his oblique and maddening way of getting to the point.

It was two things, really. It turns out that in the absence of an indigenous soul a quite separate divine spark does still reside in every new life. It's not the same as a soul but a kind of prerequisite, as it were … anyway, when we started introducing the Slelani souls it seems that they carried a Slelani divine spark with them and there was a kind of … fusion, I suppose. Resulting in something quite new, unprecedented, quite unprecedented.

And then there's the other thing … Gebril should have mentioned that the Slelani were the most nosy and curious beings in the known universe. On their world it never took them anywhere because they were just too lazy. They either understood it and lost interest, or didn't and gave up and lost interest. But combined with the humans … oh dear, oh dear, oh dear. I'm afraid I took my eye off the ball again.

Ahuv would have rolled his eyes heavenwards if it wasn't for the fact that he was already there. His self-control faltered.

AND? AND? WHAT EXACTLY, PRECISELY, SPECIFICALLY, IS THE PROBLEM!

Ashriel looked startled and then abashed.

Sorry! I'm coming to that. From the moment we started using the Slelani souls not only did the humans become doubly as inquisitive as they were before – and believe me, they were the nosiest entities I had ever come across until I found out about the Slelani - but they started to become more interested in … well, spiritual matters generally, really … I did notice it after a while but it seemed a good development – wouldn't any angel have thought that? So I rather, um, sort of left them to it, really. Their numbers stabilised and the whole expanding population thing seemed to have been taken care of …

Ahuv's wings were trembling with impatience and Ashriel recoiled from the force of his response.

WHAT. EXACTLY. IS. THE. PROBLEM. TELL ME NOW! INSTANTLY!

Well, you see, they've, um, sort of, um, found us.

Ahuv looked at him blankly.

Found us? FOUND US? What does that mean? For Heaven's sake (sorry) explain!

They both froze as a sound intruded into the silent whiteness around them. *A sound.* That was impossible. Other than any sound made by them, the angels dwelt in a warm all-embracing swaddling glow of whiteness and majestic silence.

But there it was, nonetheless. A sort of low, humming thrumming sound unlike anything they had heard before. And it was becoming perceptibly louder.

Now angels are in the rather odd position of theoretically knowing everything, but that was not exactly how it worked. It would be more accurate to say that they could know anything. If they turned their minds to it. As one the two angels cast out for the meaning of this bizarre intrusion and froze again in disbelief.

The fluffy eddying white mists all around them drifted lazily apart as a large sphere edged towards them. It was made of some silvery substance and was surrounded by a pale glowing force field. Two figures in bulky silver-coloured clothing with helmets and visors peered curiously at them through a big bubble of clear material that covered a third of the sphere. The figures turned to each other, raised an arm each and banged their hands together, jumping up and down like lunatics.

There was bold blue lettering on the side of the sphere. It read

**NASA
ICARUS MISSION**

Best Served Cold

Revenge is sweet and not fattening.

Alfred Hitchcock

Hugo's voice was insistent and enthusiastic, two of his less likeable qualities.

'Don't be such a drag, Nick! You've got to come! You know what Tommy's parties are like and I need a wingman!'

I did know what Tommy's parties were like and I had to admit that some of them had been memorable. And there were always a lot of unattached women … he was right. I had been feeling odd lately, not down in the dumps exactly, just somehow bored with everything. It wasn't even that exactly. I couldn't quite put a finger on it. Just … odd. Nothing had really changed in my life and yet it was as if something were dislocated, out of kilter. I nodded and rolled my eyes as I do whenever I realise I am pointlessly using gestures while on the phone.

'Ok, Ok, I'll come. See you there, around nine?' Hugo rang off, happy with his mission accomplished. I pottered around getting myself ready and trying to psych myself up into a party mood. It didn't really work. I was ready early and sat in an armchair staring into space, in hold mode while I waited for my cab to arrive. I tried to shake off the lassitude that seemed to come upon me more and more frequently these days, telling myself I was luckier than most. Decent flat in Bayswater, decent car, a job that was well-paid and not too demanding. No girlfriend right now, but that wasn't what worried me. Another one always seemed to come along eventually without much conscious effort on my part.

My mobile rang and I put away my musings and went down to the taxi.

Laid back and tasteful jazz murmured in the

background, low and breathy saxophone notes washing over the twenty or so people sipping champagne in Tommy's mansion flat. A few had spilled out on to his terrace to enjoy the unusually warm summer's evening. It was twilight, and I felt the melancholy I always do in that brief and other-worldly interval between day and night. Tommy rushed up and thrust a glass into my hand, slapping my shoulder hard enough to make me wince.

'Good to see you, Nick! Hugo tells me you're turning into a stick-in-the–mud these days and I thought you might not come!' I managed to side-step a friendly punch on the shoulder. You couldn't be angry with Tommy. He somehow seemed never to have grown up and his Hugh Grant floppy hair and undimmed enthusiasm for any form of hedonism were exactly the same as they had been when we were in our twenties. Thirty years on he was running to flab and there was a network of tiny thread-like red veins on his nose but otherwise he was virtually unchanged. As was his penchant for designer jackets in eye-wateringly vivid colours.

He charged off to greet another arrival and I spotted Hugo's unruly pale blonde thatch amongst the crowd and waved. He gave me a surreptitious thumbs up and rolled his eyes meaningfully at a young blonde he was chatting to. Her unnaturally large gravity-defying breasts were threatening to make a break for freedom from her very low cut, figure-hugging and clearly very expensive dress. It looked like he didn't need a wingman after all.

I sipped the champagne and nodded approvingly. Cristal, courtesy of Tommy's inexhaustible trust fund. I raised my glass to his farsighted indulgent and departed parents and wandered around aimlessly, half-heartedly checking out the women. Most of them seemed to have come off a production line somewhere in Chelsea, variations on two or three basic models. Even though a couple were really quite attractive and one of them smiled at me I just couldn't work up enough interest to make the first move. I found myself on the terrace and leaned on the railing, letting the darkening palette of greens from the garden square it overlooked soothe me into a Zen-like state.

A hand touched my arm and a voice spoke hesitantly.

'Nick? Is it really you?'

Somewhere in my head faint alarm bells went off and I turned around. She was tall, with hair that hovered tantalisingly between blonde and chestnut. Blue eyes evenly spaced over a petite nose and generous, sensuous lips looked into mine and I felt my stomach start to churn. I opened my mouth and nothing came out. The glass fell from my hand and shattered on the tiled terrace floor.

I stepped back and muttered something incoherent about cleaning up the mess and bolted. I practically ran to the bathroom, locked the door and sat on the closed loo, gulping air as if I was having an asthma attack. I don't have asthma.

It was her. My God. After twenty nine years it was her and I was behaving like a love-struck teenager. Josephine. Jo. My Jo. I staggered to my feet and gripped the basin with both hands and stared at my reflection in the mirror.

I saw a slim man in his early fifties, hair in the first stages of a graceful retreat from his forehead. The same face I saw every morning in my bathroom mirror. But this face looked as pale as a shroud and the eyes were wild and staring. I don't know how long I stood there as the memories flooded through me. Flooded is the wrong word. It was like a rapid-fire series of flash photographs searing my mind one after the other at breakneck speed.

Her head thrown back and laughing at something I'd said.

Her lips against my ears, whispering I love you.

Running hand in hand down a sun-bleached beach, shrieking with laughter.

The two of us naked on a bed, limbs entwined as if we were a single organism.

One organism. That's what I had really, truly thought we were. That's what I had been so sure of that it never occurred to me for even a fleeting second that it would ever be otherwise.

There was a knock on the door and I heard Hugo asking if I was all right. I croaked something, I have no idea what, and he went away. I sat down again heavily. The dam had been breached and there was no stopping it now. More snapshots tumbled through my brain and then they slowed and became a movie. The scene was a dimly lit restaurant and what she was saying seemed like random jumbles of words and phrases and I could only hear the ones that mattered.

Too intense. Need to experience life. There's somebody else. Hope we can be friends. Somebody else. Somebody else. Somebody else. Somebody else ...

The words echoed and bounced around my skull like the thudding of a bass drum and I leaned back against the cistern. The ceramic edge dug painfully into my spine and slowly, mercifully, the mental rollercoaster faded away. On its heels came a revelatory moment of clarity.

All this time. All the girlfriends that had lasted for anything from one night to a couple of years. My feeling of somehow being disconnected from everything. Enjoying life, yes, but never quite to the full, always that niggling feeling of something missing. All of it was her doing. That moment in that restaurant over a bottle of Chianti and congealing pasta was when she changed my life and threw me away and cast me adrift.

I felt anger, no, more than that, a fury build up in me. How could I possibly have been so blind? How could I not have realised this before? How the hell could an insight that now seemed so blindingly obvious have eluded me for so long? That bloody bitch. I had loved her unreservedly and opened myself to her completely and had been utterly defenceless when she dropped her bombshell on me. A small voice piped up and told me it was nearly thirty years ago, for God's sake, and you were both young. But I slapped it down ferociously.

An icy calm came over me and I stood up, gazing unseeingly at the bathroom door with narrowed eyes. So what now?

Go out there, said the other, stronger voice. Go out there and never let anybody see any of this. Be gracious and be charming and give yourself a chance to think about what to do. An American phrase I had read somewhere floated to the surface. *Don't get mad, get even.*

When I emerged Tommy and Jo were in the hallway waiting for me. Tommy and Jo. For a fleeting and unsettling moment it was as if I had been transported back thirty years, when the three of us had been inseparable and bursting with the optimism and vigour and silliness of youth. But it only lasted a second or two. I looked at her and thought her name and it was like a flicker of fire in my chest, a flicker I was already learning to control.

They were asking me if I was all right and I was making excuses – shouldn't have drunk so much at lunchtime, just caught up with me, really sorry to dash off like that, stupid thing really and so on. Tommy looked relieved and hurried off to rejoin the party where the music had become louder and jazz had given way to thumping rock. There was a long silence as Jo and I looked at each other.

The lid was back on the bubbling cauldron of memories, and the dominant voice in my head told me to be strong and not to worry. The initial shock was past now and I was firmly in charge of my emotions.

'Are you really okay, Nick?' she said. There was such concern in her voice that I almost believed it. But I didn't. And in that instant I felt as if somebody had wrapped me in some magical, invisible suit of armour that guaranteed my immunity from her and could never be penetrated. I laughed and took her arm.

'Trust you to turn up after all these years just at the moment my lifestyle catches up with me!' I said, plucking two glasses from a tray in passing.

'My God, how long has it been?' *Twenty-nine years, eight months and three days*, the smaller voice in my head muttered. But he was very faint now.

I had never really thought much about whether I could be charming, but I suppose I was subconsciously aware that I could if I really put my mind to it. And that is what I did. I was witty. I listened with deep interest as she told me about her life. I told her self-deprecatingly about my own and embellished and invented anecdotes to make her laugh. I allowed a subtle feeling of intimacy to form around us like an invisible cocoon, laced with easy laughter and an occasional casual touch that seemed like the most natural thing in the world. And throughout the evening part of me was a disembodied observer hovering above us, dispassionately watching and whispering suggestions that only I could hear.

Pleading a fictitious early meeting the next morning, I said goodbye. We kissed on both cheeks – *mwah, mwah* - and embraced lightly. The softness of her body against mine was familiar in the way that a treasured and comfortable pair of shoes is familiar, fitting so perfectly one is hardly aware of it. My nostrils recognised and filled with the warm, subtly perfumed smell of her. I asked her out to dinner on the following evening and she accepted without hesitation.

Later I sat at home in the dark. My limbs were completely relaxed and felt moulded to the accommodating contours of my armchair. Like an interviewer perusing an applicant's CV I ran through my life and occasionally shook my head at how again and again the way it had developed had been shaped by that one event. Where before I had felt fury I now had only a cold desire for revenge. She had done this to me. She had changed my life and thrown me away like a cheap piece of clothing she no longer had use for. For no reason, without a thought for the consequences.

Dinner the next night was all I could have hoped it

would be. I took her to Ristorante Santa Lucia, the restaurant where she had dumped me. I looked it up on Google and was surprised and pleased to find it was still around and was eager to see what effect it would have on her.

The décor had been half-heartedly modernised but it was still recognisably the same place. I had persevered and overcome the owner's fractured English on the telephone, eventually getting across what I wanted and making sure we got the same table in a semi-private corner that we had had all those years ago. I arrived early and waved when I saw her come in and watched her weave her way through the tables towards me. She wore her hair shorter now, and it was darker than I remembered it. Her figure was a little fuller and all the better for it and the simple dark jersey dress clung to her curves in a way that made most men swivel their heads to follow her progress before hastily turning back to the raised eyebrows of their dinner companions.

'This is nice, Nick. Do you come here often?' she said after we had said hello and done the air-kiss thing. My stomach clenched with bitter disappointment, and yet at the same time I felt triumphantly vindicated. A part of me wanted to scream at her. *No, you bloody bitch, this is where you ruined my life twenty nine years ago! And you don't even remember it!* But I just smiled and shook my head and said a friend had recommended it. We sat and ate and drank and talked until we looked up and realised everyone else had gone and the waiters were ostentatiously starting to upend chairs on tables and sweep the floor. We laughed and I paid and we stood on the pavement and looked at each other.

The street was dark and quiet and for once the sky was clear and a few stars were visible despite London's background glow. We stood in silence and gazed at them as we had often done long ago, lost in our respective thoughts, before dropping our eyes and looking at each other. She reached out and took my hand in hers.

'That was lovely, Nick. I really mean it. Back in there … and now … it feels like it was all yesterday.'

Oh no it doesn't, the voice inside me snarled. *Oh no it bloody doesn't.*

'Come back to my place,' I said. I hadn't planned to say it but the words just came out of my mouth. Her eyes widened and her hand tightened on mine.

'Nick, do you really think that's a good idea?' I grinned my most devil-may-care grin.

'Probably not. But do it anyway.' She looked at me for a long moment and then threw her head back and laughed. I remembered how unreasonably happy it had always made to see her do that.

'I'm starting to remember what I liked about you,' she said. The orange light of a taxi came towards us right on cue and I waved it down. We sat in it holding hands and didn't speak again until we were in my flat, both of us still deep in our own thoughts. I busied myself opening a bottle of wine.

'Do you still like chardonnay?' I asked as I filled two glasses. Personally it had never been my favourite, but back then it was all she would drink. She smiled and her face lit up.

'I can't believe you remembered! Yes, I still do. How amazing.' She leaned forward and sipped at her glass and fixed me with those beautiful eyes. Looking into them was the same as when I felt her body against mine. So familiar and so lovely and the few laugh lines at the corners that hadn't been there before made no difference at all.

'So tell me what else you remember.' For a few seconds I looked into myself and was relieved to see I had no sense of weakening, of falling under her spell again. On the contrary, I felt a great sense of liberation, of a weight being lifted off me, and calmly and calculatingly decided to simply speak the truth. Or at least an edited selection of truths. I spoke dispassionately, looking her directly in the eyes with no hint of a smile.

'I remember everything,' I said. 'I remember the scent of you. I remember the feel of you. Your lips, your hair, your skin, your eyes, your body, everything. I remember what it felt like to make love with you. I remember how my heart would pound in my chest whenever I saw you.'

Her eyes were wide and she had her hand over her mouth and I leaned back and crossed my legs.

'Of course that was all a very, very long time ago,' I continued. 'I'm just cursed with a good memory.' There were tears forming and when the first one trickled down her cheek I felt a sort of academic satisfaction, as if a complicated experiment had produced the desired result. She put her face in her hands and now she was sobbing. I didn't move and let her cry and when she regained her composure she slumped back on the sofa.

'What happened, Nick?' she whispered. 'This evening … I was happy and laughing and it was just like we used to be … why did it stop? What happened?'

I raised my eyebrows.

'Well, it's quite simple, really. I'm surprised you have to ask. You dumped me, that's what happened. You told me you didn't love me any more and I wasn't exciting enough for you and you dumped me. Found yourself a rich boyfriend, I seem to recall. Water under the bridge, sweetheart. Don't worry about it.'

She moved closer to me on the sofa and put her hand on my arm.

'I was wrong and I was stupid and I wish to God I hadn't done it. Oh. Nick.' She put her arms around me and buried her face in my neck and I could feel her shoulders shaking and the hot trickle of her tears on my skin. And knew what I was going to do. I was going to hurt her, hurt her as badly as I possibly could. And then maybe I would be truly free.

My lovemaking was hard and brutal but she seemed to take it for ardour and passion and responded more enthusiastically than I ever remembered from the old days. I suppose we were both more experienced than we had been before. And it was unbelievably, fantastically good and served to heighten the acid bitterness of my sense of loss. And after that we became an item again. Tommy was the only one who had known us both back then and he couldn't get over it.

'I just can't believe it! The two of you together again after all those years! Nobody could understand why you split up, I mean nobody! How amazing is this!'

He went on and on until I had to tell him to put a sock in it. A week later Jo and I went to Spain together and I took her to places I had visited and liked in the intervening years. One day I pulled off the main road and drove through the harsh, parched countryside until we reached a parking lot paved in ancient asphalt, spider-webbed with carelessly tar-filled cracks crumbling under the intense heat.

'There's a monastery up there,' I told her, pointing up the mountain at whose base we had parked.

'People come here on pilgrimages. I'm afraid it's a long way up but the views are breath-taking. Are you up for it?'

Since that first night she had been unrestrained in wanting everything to be as it had been all those years ago and agreed to everything I proposed. I watched her like a biologist observing an insect under a microscope, fascinated that she could just ignore the intervening decades and not see my inner coldness and believe so easily that I was doing the same thing all over again.

I won't deny I was delighted in the way she threw herself into everything we did together, from choosing a wine to making plans and making love, and made the most of it. It was easy to enjoy our time together, all the while taking a grim pleasure in her inability to see that what she got from me was not real, that I was nothing more than an actor throwing himself into the role of a lifetime. I was letting it play out until the perfect moment when she would be at the peak of her happiness and vulnerability, just as I had been.

I imagined and re-imagined the moment when I would tell her and watch the realisation dawn. Again and again I played out the savage pleasure I would feel, watching her crumble as my cold words sank in and she finally understood. I was convinced that then and only then would I be genuinely free of my anger.

And the happier she became the more my anticipation grew.

We started up the stone steps that wound up the mountain in a seemingly endless curve. They were broad and ancient and worn concave from countless feet over the centuries and we were soon both sweating and breathing heavily. There were quite a few other people, many of them elderly and making heavy weather of the ascent. We finally stopped about two thirds of the way up and sat on a stone ledge to catch our breath and admire the view, the heat from the sun like a physical presence burning into our backs.

All the features of the landscape had been evened out by distance and the absence of shadow from the sun directly overhead. From this height the endless plain seemed flat as a billiard table, shading imperceptibly from a pale straw yellow below us to a rich deep blue in the far distance. Heat and silence enveloped us, broken only by the chirping of crickets and the laboured breathing of fellow tourists who nodded companionably as they passed us.

Jo got up and went to the edge. The steps were lined with large blocks of stone with gaps between them, like the crenellations of a castle battlement. She stood in one of the spaces and craned her neck to look down and my heart started beating faster and then everything seemed to happen in slow motion.

The dry soil under her feet crumbled away and her foot slipped and she screamed and disappeared. I got up like an automaton and went to the edge and saw that she was clinging to a desiccated bush a couple of feet down. The bush itself seemed to be clinging just as desperately to a crumbling fissure in the rock.

The ground fell away in a steep slope for a few metres and then went vertical. The cars in the car par below looked tiny and unreal and for a nanosecond I saw her plunging into the void and felt the most primitive atavistic sense of satisfaction and then I was on my belly with one hand trying to hold on to a corner of a stone block and the other reaching down to her.

I gripped her wrist and we looked into each other's eyes and in that instant it was as if some brittle, bile-filled container in my chest shattered and all the hate and hurt and anger left me and all that filled me was the unbearable thought of losing her.

'Don't let go until I tell you!' I said hoarsely. 'I'm going to try and pull you up!' But the smooth edge of the stone was powdery and my grip was slipping and I saw that the roots of the bush bearing her weight were slowly and nightmarishly pulling away from the crevice that held them one by one pop pop pop and her weight was increasing and I realised I was never going to be able to pull her up and time froze and then I felt a vice-like grip on my arm and miraculously I was being pulled slowly back and Jo was sliding upwards with her hands clamped to my arm which felt like it was going to come out of its socket and then somehow we were lying on the stone steps in each other's arms and crying and holding each other so tight I couldn't breathe.

'Jesus H Christ, buddy, that was close!' The voice was deep and American and we turned our heads. He was huge with forearms the size of my thighs and his face was ashen under the bill of his baseball cap. Two women stood behind him bulging out of their Bermuda shorts, their eyes wide with shock and their plump hands clapped over their mouths.

Loose stones were digging into my back. The sun was burning my skin like a blast furnace and my arm ached like hell. But the feel of Jo against me and the look in her eyes was the most perfect thing I had ever known. She opened her mouth to speak but I stopped her with a kiss.

'Everything's going to be all right now,' I whispered, and she heard the simple truth in my voice and returned my kiss and when we finally came up for air the Americans were already walking away, shaking their heads.

'Thank you!' I called out and the man grinned and waved and they turned and trudged up the steps.

Touch Up

Beauty and folly are old companions.

Benjamin Franklin

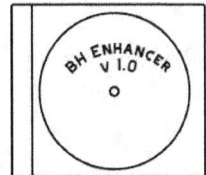

It was on the morning of her fortieth birthday that Dori first noticed a few fine lines at the corners of her eyes. She was sitting at her dressing table about to start her morning make-up ritual and had picked up her hand mirror when she saw them. She inspected them more closely and slowly put down the mirror. She sat perfectly still, her mind in a whirl. Admittedly, they were tiny. So faint as to be hardly visible. But to Dori it was as if some evil wizard had waved a wand and magicked away her youth overnight. She could almost hear him snickering cruelly.

She got up and stood in front of her full-length mirror and let her robe fall to the carpet. Her appearance was everything to her and as she inspected herself she started to feel a little better. Damn it, she did still look good. Her blonde hair cascaded to her shoulders in expensively artful curls. Her face was a perfect oval. Big blue eyes, pert nose, full lips. *Don't look too closely at the eyes.*

The bi-weekly sessions at the gym really were worth the effort. Her stomach was tight and flat and the rest of her was slim where she needed to be but with curves in all the right places. Fantastic legs even if she said so herself. Firm breasts just the right size. Even the triangle of blonde hair between her legs seemed just right, not like some women she had seen in changing rooms who seemed to have an unruly forest trying to escape from their panties.

She sat down again and mechanically went through her make-up routine. She tried to avoid looking at what she was already mentally calling crow's feet. Her phone rang and she saw it was Kimberly.

'Hi Dori, happy birthday! Really looking forward

to tonight! What are you up to today?' Kimberly was an employee of Dori's event management company in Chelsea but over the last couple of years had also become a close friend. Her only real friend. And the clients loved her.

'Hi Kimberly. Thanks.' She didn't know what to say and there was a puzzled silence at the other end.

'Dori? What's the matter? Dori?' She didn't know why but suddenly she was crying, sobbing and simultaneously furious because she didn't know why.

'Dori, you stay right there, girl, don't you move, I'll be over in fifteen.' The phone went dead and Dori stared at her reflection. This was ridiculous. She was going to have to start her make-up all over again. The tears stopped as quickly as they had started and she reached for a tissue.

*

True to her word Kimberly arrived less than fifteen minutes later. She sat beside Dori and put her arms around her.

'Tell me,' she said. 'Go on, tell Kimberly.' Dori looked at their reflections as she tried to explain what had happened. They could not have been more different and the contrast was startling. Kimberly was from South Africa and her skin was a rich deep chocolate. She was so slim she sometimes made Dori feel almost obese. She kept her jet black hair quite short and each time Dori saw her it seemed to be in some new configuration. Today it was slicked back like a Thirties Hollywood leading man and emphasised her wonderful bone structure, expressive brown eyes, and sensual mouth.

When Dori finished her somewhat incoherent

account Kimberly sat back and put her hands on her shoulders and looked her straight in the eye.

'I love you like a sister but you are one crazy white girl, you know that? I can't even see what you're talking about. You've just got the blues because turning forty has flicked some switch in that blonde head of yours. Well screw that, girlfriend. We are going shopping and then tonight we are going to party and we are going to leave a trail of guys behind us with their tongues hanging out. Got it?' Dori nodded wanly, but she was already feeling better. She always did with Kimberly.

*

A few days later they had left work and were in a pub on the Fulham Road. The owners had recently remodelled it and produced an uneasy mix of sophisticated bar and old-fashioned pub with an equally uneasy mix of locals and Sloanes. It was as if an invisible line divided the two groups who ignored each other with the studied indifference that is second nature to Londoners.

'So, girl, are you going to listen to Kimberly and try the online dating game?' Dori sighed. They were part of a loose social circle most of whom had known each other for years. Over that time the men and women in it had dated, flirted and slept with each other in almost every possible permutation. Both of them had gone out with the few they found attractive but it had never come to anything. Dori was preoccupied with making a success of her company and hadn't had anything resembling a boyfriend for over six months. By contrast Kimberly was out on a constant stream of dates and had been pressuring her for some time to join an online dating agency like the one she used, and she finally succumbed.

'Okay, okay, Kimbo,' she said. 'You win. I'll do it. I'm beginning to think you're right. At least you get to go out all the time. And they're so eager to get into your knickers they always try and impress you with expensive restaurants and champagne. Why not.' Kimberly beamed and hugged her.

'All right! Now you're talking! First thing, Dori, you need a photo for the site that's going to knock 'em dead. Let's have a look at what you've got.'

They put their heads together as Dori scrolled through her photos on her iPhone. Kimberly stopped her when they reached a shot someone had taken a few weeks ago at a party and emailed to her.

'That one's really good,' she said, 'it's just a pity that bloke's half in the shot.' It was a particularly flattering picture. Dori was smiling and looked ravishing in a skimpy black dress. But the man's arm and shoulders really did ruin the shot. As they mused over it they heard a voice behind them.

'Do forgive me for intruding ladies,' it said. They turned around and looked at the owner of the voice. His casual clothes were unremarkable other than the fact that they were all black and he was the most utterly nondescript man they had ever seen. His hair was neither long nor short, its colour was mid-brown and his face was bland without any distinguishing features. He could have been anything from his mid-twenties to fifties. Kimberly fixed him with a look that would have frozen a polar bear at twenty paces and raised her eyebrows.

'Yes?' she said icily.

'It's just that I was sitting there,' he said

apologetically and waved vaguely at the bar with his glass, 'and couldn't help overhearing.'

'And this has what to do with you exactly?' said Kimberly. The man smiled and it was such a sincere smile that despite herself she turned up her social thermostat a few degrees.

'I'm a software designer, you see, and I have some copies of my new program with me.' He produced a DVD in a clear plastic envelope and held it out. Dori took it from his hand despite Kimberly shaking her head vehemently. She noticed he had on an unusual signet ring with the elaborately entwined letters B and H. He seemed so sincere, somehow. Dori looked at the DVD. The label was plain white except for the words in plain black type. The man continued.

'As I said, I couldn't help overhearing, and this program could have been specifically designed for what you need. Load it up, open the picture and in a couple of seconds you can retouch the photo in any way you want. It's so easy to use it makes Photoshop look like a hammer and chisel and it's a hundred times better. So please accept it with my compliments. The name's Baz Hallward, by the way.'

He smiled and nodded, placed his glass on the bar and left, giving them a final cheery wave from the door. The two women stared at each other.

'Well what was *that!*' said Kimberly. Dori shrugged.

'Just good luck, that's all. It really *is* a good picture of me and now maybe I can retouch it. Come on, let's go back to my place and try it out.' They argued all the way back to the flat. Dori was eager to have a go but Kimberly was convinced they should throw the disk into the nearest bin.

'Well I think he was creepy! It might have some

nasty program that hijacks all your financial stuff or it might have some horrible virus that'll crash your computer! Don't take the chance, girl! Chuck it and we'll find another photo!'

But Dori had a stubborn streak once she had an idea in her head and was determined to try it out. To placate Kimberly she ran a full virus scan on the DVD before loading it onto her laptop and following the installation instructions. Moments later it opened a window with a message.

Congratulations. BH Enhancer is now installed and ready for use

She downloaded the photo from her phone and opened the program which told her to select the picture to work on. She really did look stunning in the photo. Another message popped up.

Do you want to remove the second person in the picture? Click Yes or No

Dori clicked **Yes** and the man disappeared. The background where he had been seamlessly matched the rest of the photo. Dori clapped her hands and turned to Kimberly.

'Pretty amazing, isn't it?'

Kimberly nodded.

'I have to admit, that's a lot easier and more intuitive than anything else I've ever seen. Sorry I was a bit suspicious. It's just that when something seems too good to be true it's usually just that. Wow. He'll make a fortune.'

*

Dori's experience with the online dating site was mixed. She was much more selective than Kimberly, and not just because her workload left her with less free time. Some of the men were quite presentable and a few even pleasant to be with, but none of them really clicked or made her particularly want to see them again. Her friend was at her wit's end and after a double date a few months later they had dumped their dates – a stultifyingly boring banker and a self-absorbed graphic artist - and ended up in an achingly trendy bar in Notting Hill.

'What is it about us?' asked Dori, her words slurring slightly. It was her third Martini on top of the champagne and wine their luckless dates had plied them with.

'What?' shouted Kimberly, spilling some of her wine as she leaned forward. Music with a thumping bass was pounding in the background and the chattering and braying laughter in the crowded bar had reached a deafening crescendo.

'Oh bugger this, I've had enough, come on, let's go.' They forced their way through the heaving throng to the door, ignoring several drunken attempts to buy them a drink. They staggered out into the cool night air and looked around blearily for a taxi.

'Come on let's walk up to Notting Hill Gate, We'll find a cab there,' said Kimberly and they stepped unsteadily onto a pedestrian crossing just as a silver Porsche came roaring around the corner on squealing tyres. It was over in seconds. They froze and the car braked and skidded and Dori felt herself flying through the air and that was all she could remember.

*

When she opened her eyes the first things she saw were Kimberly's big brown anxiety-filled eyes. She moved her hands and saw that one was bandaged around the wrist.

'Oh, Dori, thank God, they said you were going to be okay but you've been out of it for hours! Don't try and move, you were really lucky, only a fractured wrist and a few cuts and bruises … ' there was something in her friend's expression that gave Dori a sinking feeling.

'Are you sure? That's all?' She felt bandages around her head and face and raised her good hand to touch them. Her fingertips probed the gauze on the side of her face and she groaned at the stinging jolt of pain. She saw Kimberly's hand fly to her mouth and her expression frightened Dori.

'Kimberly! Tell me! My face … ' a handsome young Indian man in a white coat came into the room and smiled, exposing even white teeth.

'Hello! I'm Doctor Gupta. I'm very glad to see you're awake. You were in a nasty car accident but you're going to be all right. You really are very lucky, it could so easily have been so much worse. The driver didn't stop and just drove on, can you believe it. Probably drunk I should imagine.' Dori pointed a shaking finger at her face.

'And this? Am I going to be scarred? Doctor? Tell me the truth!' His smile faded and his expression answered her question before he spoke.

'Well, once you've healed up we will of course explore all the options, including plastic surgery. But I'm afraid that even though no bones were broken the tissue damage was quite extensive, and the truth is I doubt we will be able to hide it completely. I'm afraid there will always be some scarring. I'm really very sorry. We do have a good counselling service here, so if you would like … '

*

It was two months after the accident and Dori was sitting at her dressing table. She leaned forward and ran a finger along the jagged scar that started beside her right eye and travelled like an angry reddish bolt of lightning all the way down past her mouth until it tailed off on her chin. Smaller scars spread out from the large one like branches on a tree. She had been working from home as much as possible since she was released from hospital and hardly went out at all. She was just grateful that she lived in a day and age when she could work from home and order in groceries and takeaway meals and do virtually everything else online.

She had delegated contact with her clients to Kimberly who seemed to be doing fine. But her friend kept wanting to take her out and even after being rebuffed again and again still called her a couple of times a week.

Her injury had taken on a grim fascination for her and she inspected it minutely every day. She still went through the motions of her makeup but no amount of mascara could hide her disfigurement. She glanced down at her phone and on impulse picked it up and took a photo of herself. She downloaded it and opened it next to the one she had taken and manipulated for the online dating site. That seemed like an awfully long time ago.

She knew she shouldn't be doing it and that it would upset her but somehow couldn't help herself.

She stared at the two pictures and tears rolled uncontrollably down her cheeks. She clicked off the picture of her beautiful carefree unblemished self and was about to do the same with the picture she had just taken when a box popped up on the screen.

BH Enhancer is open. Do you want to fix this picture?

She frowned. She must have inadvertently started the program when she opened the pictures. She was about to click No but some impulse made her choose Yes. The picture flickered and the scar was gone. She smiled despite the tears as she saw herself as she was right now, looking neat and presentable and ... that was amazing! The horrible scar was gone as if it had never been.

She looked up into the mirror and screamed. The scar was gone. She was looking at her reflection in the mirror and it just wasn't there. She felt the side of her face and the knotted tissue she was so used to feeling with her fingertips like a self-torturing form of Braille was gone. Illogically she rushed to the bathroom and stared at herself in the mirror over the basin. It was still gone. She walked back to the computer as if in a trance. On the screen another box had appeared over the photograph.

BH Enhancer has saved this photo and a copy of the original

She went to the kitchen and poured herself a very large vodka and knocked it back. It burned all the way down her throat and made her feel sick and she staggered to her bed and collapsed on it. It was as if all the traumas of the past months crashed down on her at once and she sank into a deep, exhausted sleep.

It was after nine the next morning when she woke up. The curtains weren't drawn and she squinted owlishly into the sunlight, her head throbbing. God. She had slept away a whole day! Why did she drink all that vodka ... the memory came flooding back and she leaped out of bed, almost tripping and falling in her desperate eagerness to get to the mirror. She stared at her reflection. Disbelief and wild hope vied in her as she stared at her unblemished features. She looked more closely and there was definitely no trace of the scar at all. Even the dreaded crow's feet had disappeared. She reached for her phone and dialled frantically.

*

The doorbell rang half an hour later. She hadn't moved from in front of the mirror and waited until Kimberly had used her key and let herself in and hurried into the bedroom.

'Dori! What's up, girl, are you okay? You sounded so weird ... ' Dori stood up and turned around and faced her friend. Kimberly's eyes widened and her mouth was an "O" of amazement as she stepped closer and stroked the side of Dori's face.

'Oh my God. *Oh my God!* Oh Dori. Oh thank God, oh how wonderful! I can't believe it. It's fantastic. You can't see a thing. Not a damn thing!' She impulsively threw her arms around her and hugged her so tightly Dori could hardly breathe. When she eventually let her go she took her by the hand and sat them both down on the bed.

'How did you manage it? You found someone

who could fix it and you didn't tell me? And it's all healed up and it's just amazing, it's as if nothing had ever happened! Dori, why didn't you let me help you? You didn't have to go through this alone!'

Dori was about to tell her what had happened when she realised how it would sound. So she made up a story about having met this surgeon who had a new unauthorised experimental procedure and had treated her on condition she swore not to reveal his name. She could see Kimberly found it very odd, but it was the best she could come up with on the fly and eventually her friend seemed to accept it.

*

Dori felt as if she had been given a new lease of life and threw herself back into her work. And not just her work. She started going out both with and without Kimberly more and more often and was drinking too much and had several unmemorable one night stands. Every moment of her life seemed to be filled with no time left for relaxing or the long, easy-going lunches the two of them used to enjoy so much.

She inspected herself obsessively in the mirror every morning – she was usually too drunk by the time she got home at night to do anything other than collapse into bed. But despite what Kimberly called "burning the candle at both ends" she looked fantastic. One morning a little less than a year after her accident she had completed her ritual morning inspection and was on her laptop checking out her emails and schedule for the day when a box popped up on the screen.

BH Enhancer has an important message for you.

Please click OK to view.

She froze. She had tried to push what had happened that day to the back of her mind. It was so utterly inexplicable that she had a visceral dread of having anything to do with the program and did her best to push it all to the back of her mind. Being busy and out all the time had helped and she had never opened the program again since that life-changing morning. But she had already clicked **OK** before she realised what she was doing.

The photograph that opened was the miraculously scar-free photo she had taken on that memorable morning. At first glance it was as she remembered it but without any action on her part the photo enlarged until her face filled the screen and as the picture changed she recoiled in speechless horror.

There was a puffiness to her fine features that she had never seen before. Her complexion was blotchy and there were dark bags under her eyes. And worst of all the scar was there again, a livid streak down the side of her face. As she watched the photo seemed to blur momentarily and then it was back as it had been on that wonderful morning. Her shoulders sagged with relief. It must have been a momentary hallucination. Or maybe some glitch in the program. A box appeared. This one was large and had more text in it than the others before it.

Please note that your free trial period will expire in 7 days. We hope you have enjoyed the many unique benefits of using BH Enhancer and are satisfied with our product.

Please click Renew to subscribe for another year. Payment instructions will follow.

Please note that if you choose Do Not Renew all material that has been altered using BH Enhancer will revert to its current state as just demonstrated.

Dori stared disbelievingly at the screen. The words *all material that has been altered using BH Enhancer will revert to its current state as just demonstrated* buzzed around her head like an angry bee and she couldn't shake the image of the way she had looked before the photo changed back. She clicked **Renew**.

For a moment nothing happened. Then another box appeared.

Thank you for renewing BH Enhancer. Click Continue to proceed to the payments page.

Dori did so. Instead of the usual request for credit card details that she was expecting a full screen of text appeared.

Dear Subscriber

Each time you renew BH Enhancer you will be required to perform a simple task. Please follow these instructions exactly. If they are not followed to the letter or if there are any variations or omissions or if the instructions are only partially completed before the expiry of your current subscription period at midnight 7 days from today your subscription will be terminated without further notice.

In this event it will not be possible to renew at a later date. The DVD with the original program will no longer function and it will not be possible to reload the program or recommence your subscription by any other means. Please read the following instructions carefully and carry them out within the 7 day time frame. We suggest you make whatever notes you feel necessary as this page will close after ten minutes have elapsed. It will not print.

Nor will it re-open once closed.

<u>INSTRUCTIONS</u>

Place £10,000 in cash in an envelope and seal it.

Take the envelope to the place you were given the original DVD.

Hand it over to the appropriate person.

Your subscription will be automatically renewed.

We thank you again for choosing to renew BH Enhancer.

Dori stared at the screen and then scrabbled for a piece of pare and a pen. She scribbled *£10,000 cash – Fulham Road pub – seven days*. She sat unmoving and eight minutes later the box disappeared.

She spent the rest of the day going through her tasks and appointments on auto-pilot. All she could think of was the way she had looked in that picture before it reverted to the way she looked now. After a sleepless night she went to her bank and arranged to pick up £10,000 in cash the next day, ignoring the inquisitive looks from her 'Personal Banking Representative.' It was a lot of money, a hell of a lot of money, but thankfully she could afford it.

At lunchtime the next day she picked up the cash and took a taxi to the pub on the Fulham Road. She walked in and there was the man – what had he said his name was? Baz something? - sitting at the bar. She held out the envelope and he smiled and took it from her hand. He put down his glass and left without a word. All at once the absurdity of the whole situation struck her and she ran outside after him. There were only a few pedestrians but he was not one of them and was nowhere to be seen.

When she got home that evening and switched on her laptop a box popped up.

Thank you for renewing your subscription to BH Enhancer

A few seconds later it disappeared.

*

The next year was a whirl of activity. She took on new clients, some of them household names, and organised one event after the other, each bigger and more elaborate than the one before. Her confidence in her abilities and appearance grew with each passing day and her social life became more and more frenetic. Through one client, an advertising agency, she met several interesting and creative men and slept with three of them. One introduced her to cocaine and she added that to her ever-increasing intake of vodka and champagne.

In the meantime Kimberly had finally found a steady boyfriend, a quiet, unassuming and successful set designer for a British film studio, and was blissfully happy in their new relationship. She tried to maintain her friendship with Dori but couldn't stop herself warning her that she would burn out and crash if she carried on her current lifestyle. It all came to a head after a staff meeting one day. Kimberly stayed after the others had gone and tried to put her arms around Dori's shoulder.

'Dori, please. Won't you listen to me? Please? All I'm saying is ... ' Dori shrugged off her arm and rounded on her.

'Oh for Christ's sake put a sock in it, Kimbo. That's all I ever hear from you these days. Take it easy, you'll burn out, don't drink so much – look at me, woman! Do I look like someone who's burning out? I look fantastic and I can handle it so give it a bloody rest, will you? You're not my mother and I don't need this whining crap all the time. You're just jealous because you've tied yourself down and I'm partying the way you used to! So just bugger off and leave me alone! I haven't got time for this bullshit.'

Kimberly looked at her for a long time, her expression sad and resigned.

'I'm sorry, Dori, I can't do this any more. You've become someone else and I can't seem to get through to you. You're a train wreck waiting to happen and I don't want to stay around and watch it. I'm leaving now, and I won't be back. I'm so very sorry, Dori. Goodbye.' With that she left the room. Through the glass partition Dori watched her disappear and come back with a cardboard box and scoop her possessions from her desk and drawers into it. She left without a backward glance.

Dori felt empty inside. She was on the verge of running after her when the phone rang. She picked it up and it was her client and occasional lover David from the advertising agency. Moments later she was discussing their next event and laughing and joking and she pushed Kimberly to the back of her mind.

*

It was exactly a year since the last message and she switched on her laptop with a sick feeling in her stomach. The £10,000 had been painful but not disastrous and she just wanted to get it over with. She suspected it would be more this time but had made certain she had ample funds available. Sure enough the message box popped up again.

Please note that your current subscription will expire

in 7 days. We hope you have enjoyed the many unique benefits of using BH Enhancer and are satisfied with our product.

Please click Renew to subscribe for another year. Payment instructions will follow.

Please note that if you choose Do Not Renew all material that has been altered using BH Enhancer will revert to its current state as per the following demonstration.

As before the words *all material that has been altered using BH Enhancer will revert to its current state as per the following demonstration* made her feel dizzy with apprehension. As if in response to this the photo popped up and the message minimised itself to the bottom of the screen. Dori stared at it in horror and as before it expanded to a close up of her face. The scar had faded slightly but her features seemed to have coarsened and there were pronounced lines by her eyes and on her forehead. She had put on weight and her eyes were bloodshot and the bags under her eyes had turned to pouches. She looked dissolute and bad-tempered and as if she had aged far more than just a year.

She clicked on the **Renew** button. As before a page with the same preamble came up but this time the instructions were different.

INSTRUCTIONS
There is a manuscript entitled Why God Is Dead And What To Do About It with JC Publications of Wardour Street. They have recently rejected it. Obtain an interview with Managing Director Jonathon Green at the above company and ensure the manuscript is published.

The methods you use to achieve this are entirely up to you.

The publication of this manuscript must be agreed in

principle before the expiry of your current subscription period at midnight 7 days from today or your subscription will be terminated without further notice.

Upon successfully completing this task your subscription will be automatically renewed.

We thank you again for choosing to renew BH Enhancer.

Dori had a pen and paper ready this time and hurriedly wrote down the details. Moments later the window closed. She sat absolutely still. She had been expecting another demand for money and business was so good she was becoming quite wealthy. But now the money meant nothing. How on earth was she going to do this?

There was a brief moment when the old Dori she had once been before the accident surfaced and asked her what the hell she thought she was doing. A brief moment when the thought of her behaviour and lifestyle made her cringe and wonder if she was losing her mind. But the picture of her she had just seen was seared into her brain and she knew deep down with unshakeable certainty that if she didn't comply she would wake up in seven days and that was what she would look like.

*

It had taken all her experience and charm to get past Jonathon Green's secretary and persuade him to see her. She had finally arranged a meeting in two days which only left four days after that to achieve her goal. She spent the 48 hours agonising and racking her brains for some plan to persuade a publisher who didn't know her to publish a manuscript she knew nothing about except for the title and to agree to it within four days of their meeting.

She carefully sniffed a line of cocaine before setting off. Just one to give her the boost she needed. She had come to depend on it to give her an edge in tough negotiations and as the drug spread through her system her uncertainty evaporated. She felt energised and suddenly confident that she would manage this somehow.

JC Publications was on the third floor of a grimy thirties office block and she was kept waiting for half an hour before the receptionist ushered her into the Managing Director's office. The furniture was old but of good quality, some of it antique, and framed book covers lined the walls. Jonathon Green stood up and shook her hand and waved her to a seat. His palm was damp and she surreptitiously wiped her hand on her dress.

'So, Miss Grey, what can I do for you?' he said. His eyes roamed unashamedly over her and lingered on her long legs. She had worn a provocatively low-cut blouse and short skirt and saw that it was having the desired effect. He was an imposing man just starting to run to fat, over six feet tall with long wavy black hair. His face would have been handsome but for overly large lips that would have looked more appropriate on a woman. Dori forced herself to smile her most charming smile.

'I have rather an unusual request,' she began, and he waited for her to continue. There was nothing else for it and she plunged ahead.

'I believe you recently rejected a manuscript entitled *Why God Is Dead And What To Do About It*,' she said, and his eyebrows shot up in surprise. 'Well, I'm here to persuade you to change your mind.' He stared at her in disbelief.

'Surely you can't be serious. Is this some kind of a joke?' She stopped smiling and leaned forward earnestly.

'Mr Green. I am deadly serious. Would you indulge me and tell me why you rejected it?' He managed to tear his eyes away from her cleavage and stared at her.

'Miss Grey, have you read it? I doubt it. If you had I can't think that you would imagine any publisher in his right mind would have anything to do with it. It's the most scurrilous and subversive attack on religion in general and Christianity in particular that I have ever come across. What could conceivably make you want to promote this piece of trash?'

Dori saw that there was no hope at all of persuading him by any conventional means. She looked at him and in a flash of intuition knew what she had to do.

'Mr Green. May I call you Jonathon? Oh good. My friends call me Dori. I cannot tell you why but I need, absolutely need, this manuscript to be published. And moreover the publication *must* be approved in the next four days. My life virtually depends on it. Is there nothing I can say … or do … to persuade you?'

He started shaking his head and she got up and went around the desk. She leaned over him, only inches away. His eyes were glued to her half-exposed breasts and she could see a sheen of perspiration on his forehead. She put a hand on his arm.

'Jonathon. Please listen carefully because I want you to understand me. I will do absolutely anything if you do this for me. I mean that in the most literal sense. For six months I will be available to you for anything that you want from me without limit. *Anything.* Do you understand?' She didn't know where the six months had come from. But some intuition told her that less would not be enough and more was unnecessary.

He was breathing heavily and she noticed with a trace of amusement that he was becoming noticeably aroused. And knew she had won.

*

Ten years had passed. Jonathon had been a pig and at first she would go home and scrub herself raw under the shower in a futile attempt to make herself feel clean again. But the next morning she would take a photo, download and open it, and the program would come up with the magic phrase

BH Enhancer is open. Do you want to fix this picture?

And no matter how bruised or battered she had been or what he did to her or she did to herself her skin was always clear and unmarked and any pain evaporated as soon as she had clicked **Yes**. By the end of that year she had become inured to it and when she left him on the morning of the day the six months were up his pleading and tears were music to her ears.

She sat at home alone that evening, a very rare event these days. But tomorrow was the day she would find out what her next task would be. She stood naked in front of her mirror and her body and face looked exactly as it had all those years ago, before her life changed forever. She sipped the Cristal champagne that had become what she thought of as her favourite soft drink and reclined on her bed. She munched her way through the box of expensive hand-made chocolates which had become another of her growing number of addictions. The things she had done in the intervening years drifted through her mind like scenes from a play, remote and almost unreal.

None had been quite as bad as Jonathon, thankfully. There was that senior banker she had ruined, but it wasn't her fault he couldn't handle it and took his life afterwards. Spineless, that's what he was. The burglary that other time had been exciting and she had actually enjoyed the planning as much as the intoxicating high of getting away with a fabulous diamond necklace. Pity she hadn't been able to keep it. And then there was ... she shook herself and shrugged. The champagne glass fell from her fingers and the room began to spin. She really shouldn't have snorted coke with Matt earlier. She giggled. He really was such a bad boy. But fun ...

Her alarm shrilled and she groaned and switched it off. Christ. It was morning already. Well, today was the day. Again. She wondered what it would be this time and felt a little frisson of anticipation mixed with fear. Moments later the computer was on and her picture opened, enlarging and filling the screen. Even though she had steeled herself Dori couldn't stop a hiss of horror when she saw what she had become. What she would be again if she didn't perform. She quickly clicked her way to the instruction page, pen and paper at the ready.

INSTRUCTIONS
Kill somebody you know personally.
The method and choice of subject are entirely up to you.
The act must be completed before the expiry of your

current subscription period at midnight 7 days from today or your subscription will be terminated without further notice.

Upon successfully completing this task your subscription will be automatically renewed.

We thank you again for choosing to renew BH Enhancer.

She sat there stunned until the instructions disappeared. *Kill somebody.* It did not occur to her to even think of refusing. To become the awful creature in the picture was unthinkable. She shuddered. Kill somebody. *Somebody you know.* Christ. *How?* Oh God. And *who?* Seven days. She had seven days.

She bathed and dressed like an automaton and sat in her office sipping a strong double espresso as she surveyed her employees through the glass walls.

There was Gilda, the receptionist with the annoying nasal voice. Or that creep Otto from Accounts who was always undressing her with his eyes. But he was reliable and damn good at his job. She ran through her dozen or so employees but nobody seemed to stand out. There was Belinda, her PA since Kimberly left. She was good at her job too, but had an irritating watchful quality that sometimes got on her nerves.

Bloody Kimberly. Always criticising. Good riddance to her. She had heard on the grapevine that her ex-friend had married the scenery designer boyfriend, but it hadn't worked out and they had apparently split up a few years ago. That was the last piece of gossip that had chanced her way. Kimberly? No, no, what was the matter with her. What was she thinking? They had been friends. But it had to be somebody. It *had* to be. And she had walked out on her, hadn't she. After all those years just upped sticks and buggered off. Betrayed her trust, really when you come to think about it. Hmmm. Kimberly …

No, damn it … Jonathon! Perfect! If ever there was a nasty piece of work who didn't deserve to live it was that greasy pig after what she'd had to go through. The more she thought about it the more perfect he seemed. She hadn't seen him in almost ten years so nobody would make the connection. And he had always met her in his office after hours so his fiancée wouldn't suspect. And he had given her a key which she still had somewhere …

She grabbed her bag and ran out of the office and hailed a cab. She burst into her apartment and started frantically pulling out drawers until she saw it, an unmarked Yale key tarnished with disuse. She held it up triumphantly. The next thing to decide was how. She wished she had a pistol of some kind but finding one at short notice was bound to be risky. And a shot might be heard. And in any case she hadn't the foggiest idea of how to get one and certainly couldn't ask around.

She left and hailed another cab and had him take her first to her bank and then to Church Street off the Edgware Road. She prowled the three floors of the antique market until she found what she was looking for. The owner of the cramped unit smiled when she picked up an antique stiletto.

'You have a good eye, Madam. All steel, beautiful floral chasing on the handle, Italian, around 1650. Quite a rare piece, classic design. Are you a collector?' Dori put on her warmest, most I-am-only-a-woman-who-doesn't-know-about-these-things voice and made up a story about having met a man who collected and wanting to give it to him as a birthday present. They haggled politely and she eventually handed over the £900 he grudgingly let himself be beaten down to.

The next day she rang JC Publications from a pay phone and asked for Jonathon Green. The receptionist said he was busy and Dori hung up. Good. So he was still there. She sat by the window in a coffee shop opposite his office and waited. She wore her plainest clothes with her hair tucked up under a scarf and glasses she didn't need. Soon after five thirty a group of people emerged and she recognised his secretary even though she had put on God knows how many pounds since she had last seen her.

She waited for a few more minutes and casually left the coffee shop. She walked down the road for a few hundred yards, crossed it, and came back up the other side to the office door. She had the key ready and seconds later was inside and closing the door behind her. The hallway and stairs hadn't been redecorated since she was last here and it was all looking very down at heel. Cheap bastard. Well, he was going to get what was coming to him.

She climbed the narrow stairs to his office on the second floor and stood on the landing, listening. She couldn't hear anything so she turned the doorknob very slowly and opened the door. He was sitting at his desk holding a manuscript in his pudgy fingers and looked up, his mouth slack with surprise. He had grown jowls and rolls of fat bulged over his collar.

'Hello, Jonathon,' she said. She had her hand in her pocket and the handle of the stiletto was cool and deadly in the palm of her hand. Its blade had easily sliced a hole in the lining and she could feel its length against her thigh. He lumbered to his feet and came around the desk. His surprise had given way to a reminiscing smile and Dori's eyes widened with astonishment. He actually thinks I've come back to him, she thought with disbelief. He held his arms out with a lecherous grin and she stepped towards him.

The blade slid into him amazingly easily and he made a funny surprised little "Oh!" sound. Jonathon's arms were around her and he slowly toppled forward with all his weight. She couldn't escape his bear hug and fell backwards and there was a blinding pain at the back of her head and then nothing.

*

The first thing she saw when she opened her eyes was a familiar face. Familiar and yet different. There was a dusting of grey in Kimberly's hair now, and her face had lines and a serenity that had not been there before. Dori stretched out a hand and found it was shaking.

'Kimberly?' she croaked. Her friend clasped her hands in hers and her smile of relief made her look just like the Kimberly she remembered from so long ago.

'Oh, Dori! Finally! Gilda still had my number and called me! I've been so worried about you! You just wait here and don't move! I'll get the doctor.' She squeezed her hand and ran out of the door. Dori lay back and realised she was in a hospital. The back of her head throbbed and made thinking difficult. The curtains weren't drawn and from the blackness outside she knew it must be night.

Kimberly came back with a distinguished looking

man in a white coat followed by a nurse. He pulled up a chair and held Dori's wrist while he took her pulse and scrutinised her closely. He laid her hand back on the cover and sat back and folded his arms. Kimberly and the nurse stood behind him, smiling at Dori encouragingly.

'Well, Miss Grey, I don't mind telling you we were worried there for a while. You've been unconscious – borderline coma, actually - for rather a long time. I have to say you seem to be in first class shape for a woman of your age and I'm sure that contributed considerably to your recovery.'

Fragmentary memories of the events at Jonathon's office were starting to come back to her, and with them a rising wave of disquiet. The doctor was still talking.

'You'll be happy to know that your friend Mr Green seems to have responded to surgery but hasn't regained consciousness yet. But we're cautiously optimistic. I don't know what happened and I don't need to know, but I'm afraid the police are rather keen to talk to you. But don't worry, I can and will put them off until much later. Right now all we need you to do is rest. Quite frankly if Mr Green's assistant hadn't returned when he did – apparently Mr Green had asked him to get him a sandwich - it might all have ended rather differently.'

Alarm bells were going off in Dori's head as what the doctor was saying sank in. Not dead. Responded to surgery. Cautiously optimistic. Oh God! She had failed! No, this couldn't be happening! Her eyes flew up to the utilitarian clock on the wall. It was exactly midnight and another thought struck her. She reached out and clasped the doctor's sleeve in a vise-like grip.

'What day is it! How long have I been unconscious? *How long! Tell me!*' The doctor managed to disengage himself from her and patted her hand soothingly.

'There, there, Miss Grey, you mustn't excite yourself. You've been unconscious for five days since you were found and today is Thursday.' He glanced up at the clock just as the minute hand clicked past the vertical.

'Well, Friday now,' he said with a smile. The smile suddenly disappeared and he stood up abruptly, knocking his chair over backwards with a loud clatter. He was staring at her and he passed a hand over his eyes.

'Miss Grey! Good lord! What on earth is happening to you … ' he ran out of the room calling for an emergency team. The nurse was standing frozen like a statue with an expression of horror and both hands covering her mouth. Dori suddenly felt very cold. She lifted up her hands and they seemed to swell and dimple before her eyes. She clawed her way out of the bedcovers and staggered to the mirror fixed over a basin in the corner and shrieked but all that came out was a hoarse gasping croak.

Her face seemed to be swelling and puffing up in front of her eyes which were red-rimmed and bloodshot over dark pouches the colour of a ripe bruise. Her hair was lank and stringy and a jagged line of gnarled pink scar tissue was appearing on the side of her face.

She finally found her voice and started screaming and couldn't stop and her screams merged with those coming from Kimberly and the nurse behind her.

In Bad Odour

I judge people on how they smell, not how they look.

Jennifer Lopez

Susan glanced at her watch and saw that she needed to hurry if she was going to catch her bus. She opened her handbag and went through her usual mental checklist. The little screw-topped jar with the perfume-soaked handkerchief was a) there, and b) tightly closed. She opened the little silver snuff box that had belonged to her grandfather. It seemed both appropriate and ironic that this was where she kept her nose plugs. She took them out and carefully inserted one into each nostril, making sure they were seated deep and firm and that she had her set of spares. She replaced the little box, zipped her bag, shrugged on her coat and headed for the door.

She glanced at herself in the hallway mirror and studied the pale, dark-haired woman who looked back at her. She always felt she had a hunted look, but others didn't seem to notice it. Not that there were that many others. She lingered for a last moment and trailed her fingers across the surface of Jeff's photo. She kept it by the door so that she wouldn't see it constantly during her long and solitary evenings and weekends. The memory was still too raw. She turned and hurried on her way.

The swaying motion of the bus lulled her and the images of the day her life had changed forever returned, taking her unawares as they so often did. She sometimes felt as if the memory was a sort of mental predator, lurking and biding its time until its prey was vulnerable before pouncing. She closed her eyes and leaned back. There was no use fighting it. You couldn't make yourself *not* think about something once you had thought of it. It would run its course as it always did.

*

She and Jeff had been together for a year when they got married, the happiest year of (as she thought of it) her otherwise dull and unexceptional life. The registry office marriage had been quick and efficient. Both their parents had died young and the only other people present apart from the registrar were her sister Sarah and a college friend of Jeff's who clearly disapproved of the whole idea of marriage in general and Jeff's in particular and never contacted them again.

The next day they drove off in Jeff's vintage MG, tiny and low-slung and gleaming in burnished British racing green and, as he himself referred to it, his pride and joy. She had never heard of either the car or the colour, but liked its understated elegance. The drive through France had been a dizzying delight, a whirl of small hotels and restaurants in picturesque towns and champagne and wine and above all of feeling she had finally found the right man to share her life with.

It was a sunny and cloudless day when they eventually reached the Côte d'Azure.

As they drove along a winding coast road she felt that nothing could ever be more perfect than that moment. The wind in their hair and the hot sun on their faces, the impossibly deep blue sky overhead and the sparkling burnished Mediterranean on the right and pine trees on the left filling the air with the aroma of their needles and sap. She remembered her heart feeling so full she felt she might explode with sheer happiness. As if in slow motion she turned to Jeff to share the moment and saw his eyes widen and turned her head to face the road and the lorry was looming monstrously over them and the driver's unshaven face with his mouth a wide "O" of shock and surprise and then nothing.

*

She was jolted out of her reverie as a calm and impersonal recorded woman's voice announced her stop and she hurried to get off before the doors hissed shut.

She took her time walking up familiar worn granite steps, pausing to glance at the gold letters carved deep into the Grecian lintel above marble pillars that flanked the entrance. The Aloysius Cooper Institute had been her refuge from the world for more years than she cared to remember and it was with her usual sense of relief that she entered the echoing entrance hall with its cool tiles underfoot and left the hurly-burly of London's streets behind her. She nodded to Henry the porter and entered her office, or as she thought of it with a guilty trace of pride, her domain. A moment later she was spreading out the latest ancient documents acquired by the institute and became immersed in the task of classifying and cataloguing them and tried not to think about her appointment on the following day.

*

His name was James Andrews and his office was in what had once been an imposing family home in Devonshire Street. The receptionist looked as if she had strolled in from a fashion shoot and the waiting room had been incongruously designed to look like the drawing room of a country house. She picked up a newspaper and grimaced at the headlines.

Body found in woodland

Police refuse to comment on possible link to other murders

She read a little more, but it was so gruesome that she closed the paper and put it down with a shudder. The body of a teenage girl had been found by ramblers, raped and strangled in the woods near a town with the unlikely name of Swan Bottom. How could people do such things? It seemed so far removed from her everyday life as to be incomprehensible. A few minutes later the receptionist shimmied in and directed her to the lift. It seemed to have been installed some time before World War II and creaked and shuddered alarmingly as it carried her grudgingly to the second floor.

He was in his early thirties, more or less her age, with crinkly blue eyes and short brown hair, and to her surprise she immediately felt at ease with him. They sat opposite each other in comfortable clubby leather armchairs and there was a moment's silence while they regarded each other.

'So, tell me why you think you are here today,' he said and sat back, waiting. She was nonplussed and tried to formulate an answer. Because she had made the mistake of opening up to her sister when they got tipsy after Sarah's husband left her? And Sarah had gone on and on insisting that she "seek help"? She sighed, and it came out louder and more heartfelt than she had intended.

'Well, I suppose the simple answer is that my sister kept insisting I "see someone",' she said, and saw by his slight frown that she needed to say more.

'But of course that's not what you meant. Sorry. But I've never told anyone about this and it's not easy for me.' He nodded and gestured for her to continue.

'It all started after the accident,' she began and ran through the events leading up to that terrible day and what little she remembered of the event itself. She had thought about it so much and so often that the words came fluently.

'I was taken to a hospital in Nice. When I finally regained consciousness they told me I had been in a coma and was lucky to be alive. When they told me Jeff was dead I wished I had died too, in that last perfect moment. I sometimes still do. But all that is *not* what this is about. At least I don't think so.' She paused and gathered her courage to take the plunge. This was it.

'They told me I had suffered a severe head trauma and it was a miracle my skull hadn't been smashed open, and even more of a miracle that I had survived. But my brain had apparently been really knocked about and suffered severe bruising and I was quite heavily sedated for the first week or so. And that's when I first started noticing it.'

He raised his eyebrows and cocked his head, alert now, waiting for her to get to the heart of why she was there.

'One morning the French doctor came in and as he leaned over me I noticed this really strong smell. It was overpowering and I couldn't make out what it was. I think even that first time I realised there was something unusual about it. It wasn't – isn't - just a normal smell, you see, like sweat or cigarettes or garlic, nothing like that. It's as if I am smelling a colour, as if it had a tenuous texture like smoke that I can somehow see … God, I can hear how ridiculous this sounds.' She looked at him and he shook his head.

'Just tell me whatever you can. Whatever and however you want. You can tell me anything. Please go on.' The amazing thing was that she believed him, and ploughed on.

'I tried to tell them but they would just shake their heads and say *désolé* and that there was nothing they could do. That it was some kind of hallucination that would go away as I recovered. But it never did. And it's not just that, the smell and this weird sensation of seeing colours. I … I seem to absorb emotions as well … I feel them like colours … and – and now you really will think I am stark raving mad - sometimes I even see images and get these intuitive feelings about people. And the crazy thing is that I *know* I'm right. I just *know*, deep down. I can't control it and it's so overpowering I can't go out in crowded places or be with people unless I wear nose plugs. I put them in whenever I go out.'

'Are you wearing them now?' he asked. She nodded.

'Please take them out if you can,' he said softly. She stared at him. What the hell, she thought. He may as well know everything. It was almost a relief in a way. She took out her little silver box and turned away, embarrassed to be extracting them in front of him. When she turned back he had pulled his armchair closer and was barely three or four feet way.

'So what do you smell right now? Tell me exactly, in as much detail as you can.'

She took a deep breath and closed her eyes. The smell that permeated her wasn't bad, in fact it was not unpleasant at all. She kept her eyes closed as she spoke.

'It's quite pleasant, actually. It's so hard to explain … somewhere between leather and fresh hay … oh, it's hopeless, it's not like that really, but that's the closest I can get. And it's like a sort of pale gold, with swirls of … a sort of deep blue … and … ' her mind was racing as she processed the information flooding her brain.

'You're a good man … I can tell that … but you feel frustrated and depressed at the problems you have to deal with … and you feel you will never get over her … I see a blonde, long blonde hair … very slim … she was angry and you still don't understand why she left you … '

His hand gripped her wrist quite hard, pulling her out of her reverie.

'How do you know that? Who put you up to this?' She drew back in alarm at the anger in him and all the cautious buoyancy she had started feeling at speaking freely for the first time evaporated. She shook off his hand and stood up angrily.

'I should have known better. For a moment there I almost thought … how stupid I am. Stupid, stupid, stupid. This is why I never told anybody and I was right. I'm sorry for taking up your time.'

He was on his feet as well, and they were very close. His smell had become more pungent with his anger but was already changing back to what it had been before as he calmed down. He glanced at his watch and took her hand.

'Look, I'm really sorry. That was inexcusable. Please forgive me. It's just that … what you said … it's still quite raw emotionally. Er … our time is up, I'm afraid. Please come back again and let me make amends. I could see that was very hard for you. I really would like to try and help you if I can. Honestly. Please let me try.'

His sincerity washed through her senses and she inhaled the gold that had turned a pale, sunny yellow that seemed to warm her whole body and agreed.

*

Three days later she was in the armchair again and he smiled at her. She thought he really had quite a nice smile.

'I've been thinking about you a lot,' he said. 'It's quite an extraordinary thing you've told me and I wonder if you would let me try an experiment? I promise I'm not trying to catch you out or anything like that. But I want to bring in somebody else and see what you make of them. It may help me to understand. May I?'

She was taken aback and gave herself time to think while she removed her nose plugs. She inhaled and knew at once that he was telling the truth without an ulterior motive. She nodded and he picked up the telephone beside his chair.

'Hello, Amanda? Please send in my visitor. Tell him to come straight in.' He sat back and waited with barely contained curiosity. Part of her was unsettled by being put to the test like this, but she asked herself what she would have thought if somebody had come to *her* with this story, and decided to do her best. A part of her mind realised with surprise that she also wanted to do it for *him*.

The door opened and a man in his late forties came in. He had a hawkish but good looking tanned face under a thatch of sun-bleached blond hair. He walked towards them with the aid of a cane and James shook his hand warmly.

'Charles, I know you weren't expecting to see anyone else, but this is Susan.' He pulled up a chair close to her and Charles sat down slowly, grimacing. Susan breathed in and was at once caught up in a tempestuous storm of harsh odours, a confusing mixture of terrifying bitterness and undertones of calm serenity and powerful determination. She sat back with a gasp and James nodded encouragingly.

'Tell us what you're ... er, getting,' he said. Susan's mind was spinning with a kaleidoscope of smells, colours, feelings and images that threatened to swamp her.

'Oh my God ... it's so intense ... it's dark ... smoke everywhere, and the noise! Oh God! It's horrible! The blood ... bodies ... oh your poor leg I'm so glad you didn't use that pistol but you poor man you came so close ... '

Charles' face was ashen under his tan and he looked at his friend, bewildered.

'James? What is this? Who *is* this woman? How could she possibly know ... I mean I never even told *you* how close I came to ending it all after I lost my leg! What the hell is going on?'

Later when Charles had left James sat close to her again and took both her hands in his.

'I am so sorry you had to go through that. But after that first session I found myself believing you even though my rational mind told me I was being ridiculous, that it was impossible. Will you forgive me? I just had to *know*. Charles is an old friend but I could be fairly certain you didn't know about him – he's had several operations and has been staying with friends in South Africa for a while to recuperate. He only just got back a few days ago. He was a senior policeman and just happened to be on the tube at Edgware Road when the July 7th bombings happened and his leg was a real mess. They had to amputate and he was damn lucky to survive the blast. And to find out now that he nearly killed himself when he swears he never even hinted at it to anyone … well, I just have to accept what you say is true.'

They looked into each other's eyes for a few moments without speaking and a faint smile appeared on Susan's face.

'Yes, I feel the same way,' she said. 'And I suppose I will have to stop being your patient if we are to be something else.' James looked stunned and then threw back his head and laughed,

'This is just utterly amazing. If I ever want to lie to you I'm going to have to drench myself in cologne! Dinner tomorrow?' Susan shook her head regretfully.

'I have to meet my sister. She was quite insistent. The day after?' They stood and smiled and kissed as if it was the most natural thing in the world and it took them each several minutes after they had parted to realise just how strangely spontaneous and comfortable it had felt.

*

Susan felt the beginning of a cold coming on, and wished she could just have a sandwich and maybe knock back a medicinal whisky and lie down and sleep. But Sarah had insisted on coming to see her and Susan guessed it was because she wanted to know what had happened now that she had "seen" someone.

The doorbell rang and Sarah came bustling in.

That's what she did, bustle. Susan thought she was the most unquiet person she had ever known. She pulled Susan down beside her on the small sofa and sat back expectantly. Susan looked at her and wondered how on earth they could be sisters. They were so different. Sarah was, what was the phrase, yes, generously proportioned, her hair hovering uncomfortably between brunette and mouse, her wide brown eyes her best feature. And yet the whole was not at all unattractive. She had never had any shortage of boyfriends and Susan had heard her being referred to more than once as a "a good sport." She was never quite sure what exactly that meant.

'So, how did it go? What did he say? My doctor says he has a good reputation for sorting out unusual psychological disorders. Come on, what's the matter? Cat got your tongue?'

Susan had let her older sister bully her for as long as she could remember, taking the line of least resistance to get whatever it was over with as soon as possible. She opened her mouth to tell her about her two visits and abruptly closed it again.

'He's a very nice man, Sarah, and I'm glad you persuaded me to see him. I'm grateful for your concern, I really am. But I hope you'll understand that what happens there is private, and I don't intend to discuss it with you.'

Her sister's full lips compressed into a moue of disappointment. But to Susan's surprise she let the matter lie and noticed that there was a suppressed excitement bursting to be let out that overshadowed Sarah's displeasure at her unusual resistance. Sarah rolled her eyes and then leaned forward eagerly.

'Oh well, I'm sure it will help you in the long run

and you'll get over these silly fantasies! Smelling colours! I mean, *really*, Susan. But now I have something to tell you! I've met this man and I am absolutely smitten! What do you think of that?'

Susan stared at her, noticing her pink cheeks and the expectant sparkle in her eyes.

'I'm so happy for you, Sarah!' she said, and meant it. It had been a few months since her sister's husband Alan had left her and moved away with his much younger secretary. *Such a cliché!* she had said, but Susan knew she felt hurt and lost and uncertain not being part of a Mr and Mrs team.

'His name is Robert and he works for a life assurance agency – it's assurance and not insurance, did you know that? I never did – and he's really quite amusing and we have a lot of fun. So unlike Alan, thank God! I hope you don't mind, I was dying for you to meet him and he's going to drop by to pick me up in a little while. Oh I do hope you like him! But I'm sure you will …' Susan let her prattle on, happy that Sarah had found someone. She had been irritable and even more domineering than usual since Alan left and she seemed much happier than she had been for a long time.

The doorbell rang and Sarah leaped up to answer it. The man she ushered in after a hug and a peck on the cheek was not at all what Susan had expected. He was average and bland in every way, average height, neatly trimmed thinning sandy hair, mid-grey suit, white shirt, mid-blue tie. Her first thought was that she couldn't imagine what Sarah saw in him, but when he strode forward with his hand outstretched and a winning boyish smile she supposed he wasn't as bad as all that.

'Hello! I'm Robert, as you've probably guessed! I've heard so much about you from Sarah and it's a pleasure to finally meet you!' His handshake was a little on the limp side, but on the other hand that was preferable to the bone-crushers some men seemed to feel obliged to inflict.

They chatted for a while over tea and Robert talked about how he was building up his side of the agency and how he hoped to be made a partner very soon and that unfortunately he was on the road a lot. It was all innocuous enough but even though she was happy for them Susan secretly wished they would go.

The cold she had suspected was on its way was beginning to make itself more noticeable by the minute and her throat was feeling sore and tickly and she knew that if her nose started to run she would have to take out the plugs pretty quickly or it was all going to be rather unpleasant. To her relief they stood and said they had to be going, but as she made herself smile and opened her mouth to say goodbye it happened. Out of the blue she felt a tickling sensation in her nose and her chest spasmed and an enormous sneeze erupted like a gunshot.

She turned her head at the last moment and watched her two nose plugs go shooting across the room and staggered with the unexpected force of it. Sarah steadied her and her sister's familiar dullish mix of tea and flowers and browns and pinks enveloped her. She made a huge effort to pretend that nothing had happened and turned to Robert to apologise.

The wave of black and red that engulfed her was menacing enough but the smell! Oh God, the smell! It was vile, foul and stinking and made her think of abattoirs and rotting meat and then ...

A car ... silver and sleek ... screams and curses and violence ... a sickening thud and silence ... rustling leaves ...

Susan collapsed on the floor, barely conscious. All she could think about was that they must go, now, at once. She couldn't bear the ghastly assault on her senses for another second.

'Sarah! Please go, I'll be all right, just please go now!'

Her sister looked nonplussed and started to say they should stay, get a doctor, and Susan became frantic.

'No! This is my home and I want you to leave right now! *Please!* Don't fuss, I'll be all right. It's just a cold and it took me by surprise, that's all.'

Sarah and Robert still stood there irresolutely and Susan leaped up and ran to the door, wrenching it open.

'Please just GO!' she shouted with such force that her two visitors finally shuffled out and Susan slammed the door shut in her sister's shocked face. She collapsed on the sofa, stomach churning. Robert's awful reeking odour seemed to linger in the air and she ran to the bathroom and was violently sick.

She sat on the sofa sipping hot tea with lemon, having opened the windows to clear the air. She sniffed suspiciously but thankfully Robert's terrible miasma was gone and she tried very hard not to think about. The tea soothed her throat and she settled back and switched on the TV. The news was just starting and as the portentous opening music faded the camera panned to the newsreader. She was slim and Asian and very attractive and her face and voice were grave.

A police spokesman has confirmed that the body found yesterday in a Buckinghamshire wood is that of Melanie Davies, aged 16, who disappeared from her home in Swan Bottom two days ago. While also confirming that a murder investigation is underway no other details have been released. Senior officers are still refusing to comment on widespread speculation linking Melanie's death to those of other teenage girls found murdered in similar circumstances in the Home Counties over the last two years. And now it's over to Alistair Johnson with the latest sports news ...

Susan switched off the TV and carefully put her tea down on a side table. She closed her eyes and sat motionless as against her will the horrible things that had washed over like a tide of sewage returned with a vengeance.

The images she had seen were like random flickers and as she grimaced at the remembered stink so more pictures flashed through her brain.

A girl's terrified face, screaming ... the rustling of dry leaves on the ground as she was dragged by the feet through ... yes, through woods ... then a frenzied tearing at the clothes and ...

There were merciful gaps. But not enough to spare her a flash of a blood-stained knife and then the maniacally mechanical clicking sound of a camera.

She sat there motionless for a very long time and when she eventually looked at her watch was startled to see that it was nine o'clock and darkness had fallen. In that time she had let her mind roam over the year since the accident. How at first her new-found ability (or disability, as she thought of it) was erratic and varied greatly in intensity. She managed to live with that for the first few weeks after being discharged from the French hospital but then her experiences started becoming more vivid and intense and the only answer she had found was to block her nasal passages completely.

Once a plug fell out and disappeared down a gutter and in desperation she had doused a handkerchief from a little vial of perfume in her handbag and that managed to block out most of the terrifying assault that came at her from all sides. So now she always carried a saturated handkerchief as well as her spare plugs to guarantee her sanity and enable her to function.

But now … she didn't know how to deal with this. An image of James came to her, of their kiss and the peace and warmth of experiencing him and she took his card out of her bag and dialled his mobile without thinking. He answered at once.

'James. Something's happened and I don't know what to do. Please can you come over? You have the address? Good. Please come quickly. Thank you. Thank you.'

Twenty minutes later she opened the door and felt his arms around her and let his essence soothe her and overlay her horrible experience. She let him sit her down on the sofa and told him everything, every detail. When she finished he looked stunned.

'My God, Susan, this is unbelievable. No, no! I don't mean that! Of course I believe you. I just mean … ' he shrugged helplessly.

'This all so incredible. You're sure in your own mind this Robert is the one who murdered that girl? Absolutely certain?' She nodded and he sat back and passed a hand over his eyes.

'What the hell are we going to do? We can't just go

to the police with this - they would be more likely to lock *us* up than him.' He thought furiously.

'What about your sister? She shouldn't be with him. And maybe if you told her she might begin to see … ' Susan shook her head.

'Sarah has always been stubborn and never wants to admit she's wrong about anything. That's why Alan leaving her hit her so hard. And if we tell her Robert is a murderer … I just don't know what she'd do. She already thinks I'm some sort of nutcase and would never believe us.' She sat up straight and looked at him.

'I don't really know anything about him – not even his surname. We need more information.' She handed James a notepad and a pencil and picked up the telephone and dialled. It rang a few times before her sister answered.

'Hello, Sarah. I just rang … yes, I know, I know. I'm so very sorry about this afternoon. It was just one of those things and I'm afraid I … yes, I know. That's why I called. I hope you're not too upset … yes, please do tell Robert I apologised when you see him … oh, he's away? An early meeting in Aylesbury? Yes, it's a pity his work takes him away … '

James could hear the indistinct voice on the other end start become calmer after its initial outraged tone. Susan looked at him and took a deep breath.

'The thing is, Sarah, just yesterday Professor Sanderson at the Institute was saying he wanted to take out some life assurance on himself and his wife, and it occurred to me this might be something that Robert could do … yes, and of course the Professor has a lot of contacts in the academic world ... so could you let me have some of Robert's details? I don't even know his surname, you see. No, please do me a favour and let me talk to the Professor before you mention it to him, all right? Then I can let him contact Robert directly … '

A few minutes later she put the telephone down and they looked at each other and then at the notepad on James' knee.

> *Robert Morton*
> *Abercrombie Life Services*
> *Procession Way, Milton Keynes*
> *Telephone : 01908 73265778*
> *Website : www.abercrombielife.co.uk*

'So what now?' said James. 'We still can't just go to the police with no evidence. And even if by some miracle they were willing to look into it they would never get a warrant.' He thought for a moment and snapped his fingers.

'Charles! Of course! He was a police officer, and he saw what you can do. I'll call him now.'

*

It seemed the most natural thing in the world for James to stay the night and Susan had never felt this way before, not even with Jeff. Charles arrived the next morning and over coffee they laid out everything that had happened. The older man sat deep in thought for some time before speaking.

'Look, Susan, no matter how fantastic all this is, I have to believe you because you saw - or smelled or whatever it is - something in me that I know for certain not a soul knew about. But James is right. I know how policemen's minds work and to go to them without a shred of evidence isn't going to get us very far. I still have quite a few friends and contacts on the force so I can help, but we need something more. Hmmm. You said this Robert works for an insurance agency … and he's out and about a lot … well, even though I'm retired, if he *is* this monster he needs to be stopped. I have an idea. There is this one man … in fact I was the one who arrested him.' He asked for the telephone, looked up a number in a dog-eared pocket diary and dialled.

'Stewart? Hello! Yes, it's Charles here. Much better thanks. No, no, I'm fine, really. Yes, I got back a few days ago. Look Stewart, I need a favour. You remember that hacker we pinched a couple of years ago? The one doing the benefit fraud? Yes, Jimmy Bartoli, skinny little nerd with long hair, that's the one. Any chance you can give me an address where I can find him? Hang on, let me get something to write with. No, it's better you don't know. I definitely owe you one and I promise I'll tell you about it soon. Thanks. Much appreciated' He put the phone down.

'Well, that's part of it. What we need now is an up to date computer with fast broadband.'

'I have all that at work,' said Susan. 'I do a lot of research online. What are you thinking? And who is this Jimmy Bartoli?'

*

The next morning she, Charles and a very subdued and resentful young man with long lank hair got out of a taxi in front of the Aloysius Cooper Institute and mounted the steps. Henry returned Susan's greeting and waved them in when she told him the two gentlemen were going help her with some research, although he did give the slouching, angry-looking Jimmy Bartoli a very doubtful look.

Once they were in Susan's office she booted up the computer on her desk and Charles pushed Jimmy firmly into her chair in front of it.

'Right now, Jimmy. You remember the little conversation we had, don't you? So the quicker you give me what I want the quicker you get your money and get to leave and never see me again.' He took out Susan's piece of paper with Robert's details and slid it across the desk.

'Now, Jimmy I want to find out everything you can about this man, do you understand? Every detail, every scrap of information, nothing is too small or trivial. I want it all. Show me what you can do.'

Jimmy snatched up the paper, glanced at it and moments later his fingers were dancing over the keyboard. Susan and Charles withdrew to a corner to let him do whatever he was doing.

'How did you persuade him to help?' she whispered. Charles smiled and Susan shivered. She knew instinctively and from what she had "seen" that he was essentially a good man, but he had a core of steel and she was very glad they were on the same side.

'Let's just say I offered him the option of a financial incentive and a new friend with contacts in the police on the one hand, and on the other a broken nose and an enemy with contacts in the police who would make it his business to make his life a misery. I think he found it quite easy to make the right choice.'

They were interrupted by a derisive snort from Jimmy.

'I'm into the agency's intranet – their security is a bloody joke. They deserve to be hacked. Okay. Robert Morton, this is your life … '

Jimmy quickly found the personnel records and Susan's laser printer started spewing out sheet after sheet. But it was when he found Robert's expense claims that they hit pay dirt. The printer spat out copies of one monthly expense claim after another while Jimmy sat back twiddling his thumbs looking sulky and bored. Charles got out his notebook and started poring over the sheets of paper.

'I rang Stewart again and made him give me a list of dates and locations for all the murders,' he said. 'He's getting very curious but I managed to stall him – for a while anyway. Right. Let's start with the first one, 15th February last year ... July ... March ... here we are.' His finger ran down the columns of the expense form and he looked up with a wolfish grin.

'Bingo. The girl was found in some waste ground behind a derelict factory off the A4010 and he has a credit card voucher from a petrol station outside Princes Risborough – which is also on the A4010 and not far away at all. Let's look at the others.'

Charles had brought a battered AA map with him and they marked and collated each of the murder dates and locations. There were eleven in total and Susan looked at Charles with a shocked expression.

'They didn't want to create a panic,' he said. 'So when the press only made a connection between three or four cases they didn't correct the impression. It's always good to keep something up your sleeve. Helps sift out the loonies.'

Jimmy cleared his throat tentatively.

'Er .... are we done here? Can I go now? What about the dosh?'

Charles took £200 from his wallet and handed it to him.

'Not bad for less than an hour's work, eh, Jimmy? Okay, be off with you then. And if you ever tell a soul about this ... '

Jimmy grabbed the cash and was out of the door before he had finished speaking. Twenty minutes later Charles and Susan were finished and looked at each other triumphantly.

'An almost perfect bloody match,' he said. 'This proves that for every single murder he's been in the general area on each specific date. And some of them have receipts from places very close by geographically and within a couple of hours in time. I think this is good enough.'

*

Susan, Charles and James were back at Susan's flat when the phone rang. It was her sister and she sounded hysterical.

'You had something to do with this, didn't you! You just couldn't bear to see me happy, could you! How could they accuse poor Robert of something like this, it's crazy, it's ridiculous, he would never ... '
Susan interrupted her.

'I'm really sorry Sarah but I'm afraid it is true and you must see I had no choice. He had to be stopped. You're welcome to come and stay with me for a while if you want ... '

Her sister slammed the phone down and the other two looked at her sympathetically.

'Hopefully she'll come around if you give her time,' said James and took her hand. The telephone rang again and she handed it to Charles, who listened silently and said, 'Thanks for letting me know,' and put it down.

'He's confessed,' he said. 'They searched his office and flat and car and found photos of each victim on his mobile. A lot of mobile cameras are programmed to make that old-fashioned shutter sound and that must have been what you heard. As soon as they showed him those he told them everything they wanted to know.' He got to his feet and picked up his cane.

'This is a wonderful thing that you've done, you know. Remember that to set against all the irritating and tedious aspects of this – well, gift, for want of a better word. I'll leave the two of you alone now.' He smiled and let himself out.

*

Six happy months passed. She gave up her flat and moved in with James and they spent as much time as they could together. She revelled in being with someone with whom she could use all her senses and not only find it pleasant but spend their time together in undreamed of levels of closeness and intimacy. Sadly her sister Sarah had not forgiven her and pig-headedly insisted that she was to blame for everything that had happened to Robert even in the face of his confession and subsequent conviction.

She had a new-found confidence that permeated everything she did and now when she looked in the mirror she no longer saw the haunted face that she now knew had just been a shadow of her true self.

She often thought about those heady couple of days and how she and only she had been able to identify a psychopath like Robert and be instrumental in bringing him to justice. Even though the experience of being exposed to Robert's true nature through his smell had been horrible, it had been worthwhile.

The doorbell rang one evening while she was waiting for James to get back from work and there stood Charles, smiling and holding out a bunch of flowers. His tan had faded but he looked much happier than the somewhat sombre figure she had first seen in James' office.

'I seem to remember you saying that ordinary everyday smells aren't a problem for you, so I hope these are okay?' He kissed her lightly on the cheek and she showed him in. When they were settled with a glass of wine each he seemed ill at ease until she sat forward and looked at him sternly.

'What's on your mind, Charles? Is something wrong? You can say anything to me, you know that.' He sighed and looked abashed.

'I'm glad you said that! Well, here goes. After the business with that animal Morton I sort of drifted into doing consultancy work for the Met – they're very big on outsourcing these days, and helping them get that maniac gave me quite a bit of kudos. I did tell Stewart – you know, my friend at the Yard who gave me the information I needed? Well. I did give him a slightly edited version of what happened and he thinks I'm probably nuts but can't deny that whatever it was, we got our man.'

Susan nodded, still not seeing what was making him uncertain or hesitant, or where he was going with all this. Charles took a deep breath.

'Morton wasn't unique, I'm sad to say. We are lucky here in that we don't get as many serial killers as they do in the US, for example. But unfortunately we do still get them. I don't know if you've seen it in the papers, but there have been three murders in the East End, all prostitutes, and we think somebody is trying to be a modern-day Jack the Ripper. They have two suspects and both them are pretty equally balanced in terms of weirdness, opportunity and so on. But there's no direct physical evidence against either of them as yet. Just tentative descriptions and suspicious behaviour. They might even both be innocent – who knows?' He cleared his throat and Susan sat back wide-eyed as it dawned on her what was coming.

'Is there any chance you would agree to er, you know, smell them and see what you can tell?' She gaped at him and shut her mouth with an audible click. She remembered the vileness of Robert's emanations and how it had made her sick and … *and how you brought a mass murderer to justice and probably saved who knows how many young girls from a terrifying death*, another voice said sternly in her head. *Wasn't that worth a few moments of nausea? Well wasn't it?*

'I'll have think about it, and talk it over with James,' she said slowly.

'Of course, of course. It's just that we only really have until tomorrow before they need to be charged or released. So could you let me know first thing?'

She nodded and Charles got to his feet with a grimace. He turned at the door and as their eyes met he smiled that slightly wolfish smile of his and in that instant she knew she would do it and saw that he knew it too.

'Pick you up around ten?' He said, and without waiting for an answer closed the door behind him.

Vindolanda

Caius Acilius Verus hated the way patricians managed to look benign and almost kindly even as they made it quite clear they wished they didn't have to deal with riff-raff like him.

This particular specimen rejoiced in the name of Lucius Fabricius Catullus and Caius had to admit grudgingly that at least he was not running to fat like so many of his fellow aristocrats. Carefully curled blond hair framed a tanned narrow face and aquiline nose. Perfect for looking down at me, he thought. The Legatus Legionis casually dropped the scroll he was reading and watched it curl up like an animal trying to hide. He looked up at Caius and smiled sadly.

'So, Centurion. Your record. Not a very happy tale recently, is it? You can understand why Numerius Cocceius is badgering me to do something about you.' He sighed and shook his head. His cold eyes wandered into the distance, exactly matching the blue of the sparkling Mediterranean sea upon which they lingered before dragging themselves back to the tedious present. Caius felt the familiar stirrings of rage that served him so well in battle and so badly in peacetime. Soft patrician bastard. Just look at his hair, those carefully contrived ringlets, and that cloak – by all the gods, it must have cost a year's pay or more. The gold thread alone ... but the Legatus was speaking again, his languid tones grating on Caius' ears.

'You're very lucky that I do so abhor wasting experienced men. Fortunately for you an old friend of mine is a Legatus Legionis in Britannia. Unfortunately for him, it's a ghastly place, by all accounts. Be that as it may, he writes that there is a cohort on the wall of Hadrian that needs a replacement centurion. Best all round if you make yourself scarce from here, wouldn't you agree? I'm sure there will be plenty of blue-painted barbarians on whom you can take out your, er, dissatisfaction. Report to the Signifer for funds and transport arrangements. You leave tomorrow. Dismissed.'

Caius saluted with his right hand in a fist over his heart and left. His face was an expressionless mask as he made his way across the dusty parade ground under the sweltering noonday sun and relived the events that had led him to this point.

*

His father Marcus Cassius was distantly related to a minor patrician family, but by a quirk of several fortuitous deaths of relatives had inherited a farm in Umbria along with properties in the capital. The combined income from the farm and rents from the overcrowded tenements in Rome's Subura district allowed him to make a comfortable and quiet life for himself, his wife Faustina and their only son, Caius. The boy grew up strong and healthy in the country air and loved all things physical. He worked and wrestled with the farmhands, rode, and even flattered and badgered the farm overseer, an ex-legionary, into teaching him how to use a sword and other basic arts of war. His parents saw no harm in it and assumed it was a childish phase that would fade as he grew older.

And so indeed it seemed. He was reasonably bright and learned his letters and read the classics when he was not out and about. Life had settled down to a safe and familiar routine and by the time he was twenty Caius was starting to take over the running of the farm from his ageing father.

They were sitting at lunch on the terrace behind the villa. The trellis overhead was heavy with leafy vines dripping with bunches of jewel-like grapes just mellowing from green to purple. Dappled sunlight cast mottled patterns on the weathered table and the remains of their lunch as the three of them sat back and relaxed. Insects droned and the fields and rolling hills in the distance were washed with noonday heat and brilliance.

Faustina suddenly gripped the table and made a strange gasping noise before clutching at her head and toppling off her chair to the floor. She was pasty white and breathing with difficulty and Caius and his father carried her inside to her bed. A slave was despatched on a horse to fetch a physician from the nearby town while they held her hands and bathed her forehead with cool water.

The doctor arrived an hour later and was led straight to the bedroom. He was a Greek and Caius and his father silently thanked the gods as the Greeks were known to be the best doctors, unlike many local charlatans who had little or no real knowledge of medicine. Caius' mother was breathing a little more easily but she did not speak and seemed to have lost the use of her arm and leg on one side. After examining her the doctor gestured to them to follow him outside.

'She has been struck down by the gods,' the Greek said after accepting a glass of wine, and raised his shoulders helplessly.

'At least that is what most people call it. Personally I believe that something happens in the brain – a burst blood vessel perhaps - to cause such a loss of abilities. But that is neither here nor there. I am afraid I have no remedy other than to suggest you try and make her use and exercise the affected limbs and speak to her often and try and make her speak no matter how hard it seems. I believe she is fully aware even though she cannot communicate. Do not lose heart. Cases such as these do sometimes recover most or even all their faculties.'

They thanked him for his honesty and sent him away with a generous payment. The foreman had been standing nearby and cleared his throat.

'Forgive me, sirs, but there is a woman in the village … well, she has helped many people and if you wish I could ask her to … ' Marcus snorted angrily.

'Not so much a healer as a sorceress if half the gossip I have heard is true. Have we come to this?' He saw the expression on his son's face and his own softened.

'Well, what harm can it do? At worst I will be a few denarii worse off and if there is the remotest chance … '

The long suffering slave was despatched on his horse again. This time it took two hours before the beast reappeared with two figures on its back. The slave dismounted and the other rider leaped athletically to the ground and strode up to them.

'I am Angerona. Where is your wife … ' she glanced at Caius and added, 'and your mother?'

His father led her into the house and Caius stood rooted to the spot. She had wild raven hair and her face and arms were a deep golden brown and the brown of her eyes was so dark they seemed an almost bottomless black. Her body moved with lithe grace under a thin worn summer robe that did little to conceal her shapely body. Caius shook himself as if from a trance and ran after them.

She was bending over his mother and repeated almost exactly what the Greek physician had said. He never knew what made him do it, but Caius stepped forward and grasped her arm.

'Is there really nothing you can do? Something that the physician cannot? Please. I beg you. If there is anything you must tell us. Anything. We will pay.'

She looked at him searchingly and Caius felt as if the world was holding its breath and the moment seemed to stretch into infinity. As if she was seeing into his soul and learning everything there was to know about him. Eventually she nodded and gently disengaged his hand from her arm.

'There are things I can attempt, but I can guarantee nothing. All I ask from you is the cost of the herbs and other things I must obtain. Beyond that I leave up to you what if anything you wish to give. But I have one condition. When I return I must be left alone with her with no interruptions until I emerge. Do you agree?'

Caius looked at his father who shrugged dispiritedly and nodded.

'Very well,' she said. 'Tell your slave to take me where I need to go and I will return as soon as I can.'

Dusk had fallen by the time the tired and by now extremely disgruntled slave brought her back. She had changed into a thicker blue robe with odd symbols around the sleeves and had a voluminous leather bag slung over her shoulder. She silently pointed to the bedroom door and Caius and his father reluctantly obeyed and left and she closed it firmly behind them.

They waited for what seemed like a very long time. They smelled burning herbs and heard incantations and chanting and then there was silence. When the doors opened Angerona looked pale and drained and was holding a cloth spotted with blood on one of her fingers.

They rushed in and Faustina was propped up on her pillows looking pale and sleepy. She smiled at them weakly.

'Marcus ... Caius ... what happened? Who was that woman? I feel so strange ... ' her eyes closed and she sank into a deep sleep. Marcus withdrew a purse from his pocket and handed it to Angerona.

'I do not know what you did but you have restored her to us. We thank you. The slave ... ' Caius interrupted him.

'I will take her back, father. It is late and I should see her safely to her home.' Marcus raised his eyebrows but his attention was on Faustina and he shrugged his assent. Caius had a fresh horse saddled, mounted, and held out his hand. A moment later she was behind him and they were cantering down the long moonlit country road, cypresses on either side casting alternating bars of inky black and silver across their path.

They rode in silence with nothing but the sound of crickets and the occasional night bird to break the absolute silence of the late night countryside. Caius was acutely aware of the warmth of her body and the softness of her breasts against his back and her arm around his waist. He kept thinking of that moment when he felt as if he was drowning in her eyes.

'I felt it too.' Her words startled him and for a moment he was unsure what she meant. He reined in the horse and turned in his saddle until his face was inches from hers.

'Did you?' he whispered. He saw her smile and then their lips met and that moment too seemed to last forever.

'Yes, I did. Now ride. It is late and I am tired.' Following her directions they eventually arrived at a modest cottage down a small lane some distance from the village. He dismounted and when she slid down from the horse their bodies met and he held her for much longer than necessary. She smiled again and took his hand and led him inside.

*

Faustina still limped and had little strength in one hand, but her speech had returned and her mind was as clear as ever. They had finished lunch and she turned to Caius and put a hand on his arm.

'I am your mother and I can tell when there is something on your mind. Tell us, Caius. We are your parents.' The young man heaved a sigh.

'It is true, mother. I do have something I want to tell you both. I am in love and I want to get married.'

His parents exchanged the sort of look couples have exchanged throughout the ages when their offspring make unexpected or unwelcome announcements.

'And who's the lucky girl?' his father asked with raised eyebrows. 'Have we met her? Why have you not told us about this before?'

'It is Angerona,' replied Caius. His parents exchanged another look and his mother turned away, gesturing to his father to respond.

'You cannot be serious. Caius. Surely you can see

that this is impossible. Fine, sow your wild oats as any young man does, but …'

'But what, father?' Caius' voice was dangerously soft.

'For Jupiter's sake, son! She's not only considerably older than you - *she's a sorceress!* Don't you understand? We may only have a tenuous connection to a very minor patrician family but we can nonetheless trace our ancestry back to the time of the Pyrrhic wars! That's nearly five hundred years! We have no idea where this woman even comes from. And SHE IS A SORCERESS! A WITCH!' His father was shouting and red in the face and his mother was looking at him pleadingly. He returned her look but there was no warmth in it.

'Do you feel the same, mother?' She held up her hands helplessly and he nodded.

'I see. I had hoped you would put my happiness before your social concerns but I see that is not to be. I am going to be with her one way or another. The choice is yours.' His father leaped to his feet and pounded the table with his fist.

'I will disinherit you, boy! If you walk out of here and do this you will be dead to this family!'

'So be it,' said Caius sadly. He went to his room and packed his belongings into two capacious saddlebags. He stood in the doorway and looked at his parents and his father turned his head away and his mother put her face in her hands but neither of them uttered a word. He turned and left.

*

That had been how it started, how his life had changed forever. His father used his not inconsiderable local influence to stop anyone offering him employment and only the very brave or desperate dared to sneak to the cottage under cover of darkness to ask for Angerona's help and risk the local patrician's displeasure. They were married in a small temple many miles from the village without any of the usual *nuptiae* celebrations, just the two of them and a reluctant but well-paid priestess.

After the initial euphoria of being together had worn off and the reality of their situation made life harder and harder day by day he started drinking too much. One night in a tavern a recruiter for the army had little difficulty in persuading him that a career as a legionary was an honourable and even exciting way out. Angerona hated the idea but saw that without the self-respect that came with a man's work he was on a downward spiral that she was unable to halt.

She followed him to his first posting and then the next and the next, living in a succession of small rooms near whatever camp he was in. Sometimes she was alone for months at a time when he was away on a campaign. But at least they were fortunate in that the centuries-old rule that legionaries could not be married had been rescinded only a few years earlier.

They were at a small garrison town in Gaul when Angerona told him she was with child. They were still there when she gave birth to twins, both girls. The midwife placed the two swaddled bundles in her arms and she touched one of the two wrinkled red faces, closing her eyes while Caius stroked her hair and wiped away the sweat of childbirth with a damp cloth. He thought he saw a flicker of disappointment cross her face and she moved her hand to the other one. Her eyes widened and she smiled.

'This one has it,' she whispered, 'but not the other one. A pity. But they are both beautiful, are they not?' He knew at once what she meant. They called them Aurora and Aurelia. The first time he was sure about Aurora was after they had turned three. He came home after stopping at a stall to buy some sweetmeats for the girls and when he stepped through the door and put his arms around them Aurora kissed him, beaming.

'Oh *Pater!* My favourite sweets! Thank you! Thank you!' He handed them over and Angerona smiled and nodded. Neither of them noticed the intense, puzzled look on Aurelia's little face.

There were still times when he had dark moods and would sit on his own drinking and his wife and children had learned to leave him alone while he worked the bitterness and black thoughts out of his system. Thoughts of his parents and of the blood and death and mutilation he had seen in battle. Aurelia would sit on the floor and say, *why is daddy angry?* and Aurora would touch his face with her hand and cover her mouth with an expression of horror with tears in her eyes. He knew that Angerona had been right and that she, like her mother, could in some unfathomable way tell what he was thinking just by touching him.

*

Caius came back to the present and entered the quartermaster's warehouse. He was issued with a heavy cloak and knee-length woollen trousers, one of the few concessions the Legions made to postings to colder climes. There was a convoy of supplies due to leave for Britannia the following day and he was to travel with it. So that was that. He left the camp to give Aurora and Aurelia the news and to tell them to be packed and ready at first light the next day.

*

The three of them stood on the stone ramparts. It was early summer so it wasn't exactly cold but the leaden skies anointed them with an unremitting and soul-deadening drizzle. Gusts of wind whipped the drops into their faces hard enough to sting and made them wrap their cloaks tightly around themselves. After parched and sun-baked Provincia the lush panoply of trees and grass and fields spread before them was a kaleidoscope of unnaturally rich and vivid shades of green. But their gaze was constantly drawn to the man-made marvel upon which they stood.

The crenellated stone wall was at least twelve feet high and stretched to the horizon in both directions as far as the eye could see, snaking over the contours as if some god had unrolled it from a massive reel and laid it carefully across the land. Regularly spaced forts and watchtowers set into the wall every Roman mile only made the undertaking more incredible and breath-taking. Caius turned to his daughters, their dark eyes wide as they drank in the unfamiliar landscape.

'Well, girls, here we are. The farthest edge of the Empire. Behind us, Rome rules all the way across Gaul, Hispania and Italia to Dacia, Mesopotamia and Africa. Before us, nothing but wilderness and barbarians.' They looked at him and then at the sea of dark trees looming in the distance like a barbarian army standing to attention, biding its time. Aurora said nothing but nodded seriously. Aurelia was bored already and shrugged with a marked lack of interest.

'Come, let's get out of this blasted rain and try and get dry and sort out our quarters.' He held out his hands and they took one each and followed him down the dripping stone steps.

They had arrived the night before after weeks of travelling with the slow convoy of supply carts across Gaul. Then there was the crossing of the grey and choppy Oceanus Britannicus before a muddy and depressing trek from Cantiacorum on the coast all the way to Vindolanda, their destination on Hadrian's Wall. Aurora seemed immune to the hardships of the journey and was endlessly fascinated by each new experience. Aurelia was withdrawn and silent, resentful of the disruption to her life. For Caius it was a bitter trek away from the centre of things, a humiliation to be endured. And every time he looked at the girls he saw their mother and replayed that awful night.

They had been in Provincia for four happy years watching the girls grow up while Angerona settled down and became well known amongst the locals for her healing powers and herbal remedies.

One night he had arrived home worse for drink after celebrating a fellow centurion's retirement. He was still some distance away when he saw that their door was not just open but hanging crookedly from one hinge and felt a sinking feeling in the pit of his stomach. He drew his gladiolus and entered as silently as he could. In the flickering light of the cooking fire he saw Angerona lying motionless on the floor in a pool of blood glistening blackly red in the firelight. A man was cursing as he pawed through the contents of a chest and another had Aurelia in an arm lock and was holding a pugio to Aurora's throat repeating

Where's the money? Where's the witch's money? in a slurred voice.

The standard-issue legionary's dagger glittered against the girl's brown skin and the next moments were a blur and then there were three bodies on the floor and he was holding the girls and they all had tears streaming down their faces. Unfortunately the two bloody corpses were no common thieves. They were off-duty legionaries and even worse one of them was a nephew of Numerius Cocceius Glabrio, a *Tribuni Angusticlavii* and Caius' immediate superior.

And so here he was at the edge of the world, nursing the simmering anger he carried around with him like a wound that never healed, and the only protector of his and Angerona's daughters, constant reminders of the only woman he had ever loved, and of a responsibility he could never shed.

*

The barracks were one of a series of long single-story buildings with rows of small rooms each housing a contubernium of eight men, the basic unit of the Roman army. The name derived from ancient times and meant 'tent group', and these units became like families, like brothers. They more or less had to in order to somehow manage to live, sleep, eat, and cook together in their cramped quarters. Altogether the ten contuburnia made up a centuria, and as centurion Caius had a room at one end to himself.

He made arrangements with a woman called Barita to look after the girls when he was on duty or had to be away, the matriarch of a family of Romanised Britons living in the vicus outside the fort who spoke passable Latin and made a good living running one of

the taverns. Barita and her husband had their hands
full with their business and Aurora soon found she
was able to slip away for ever longer periods and
explore her new surroundings. Aurelia on the other
hand preferred to stay in the vicus, playing with her
dolls.

Aurora knew she was closer to her father than
Aurelia, perhaps because she sensed a kindred soul in
their lack of a need for the company of others, a quiet
shared self-sufficiency. The fort was the standard
Roman walled oblong enclosing neat rows of barracks
and other buildings with a gate at each short end.
Outside was the haphazard huddle of the vicus, the
village populated by what she heard one legionary call
"tame" Britons alongside a few retired legionaries and
their families.

She liked the vicus with its raucous taverns and
constant comings and goings and the clanging of the
blacksmith and the stench of the tanner and the
hubbub of market days. But she had known the
towns of Provincia – Massillia, and Nemausus with its
aqueduct and huge amphitheatre - and compared to
them this was tiny and insignificant. After the first
few days she had seen everything there was to see and
started ranging further afield.

*

Caius was trying to get to know the men of his
century and assess them. The garrison was the Cohors
IV Gallorum, the 4th Cohort of Gauls, a little under
five hundred men. Their accents were atrocious,
almost as bad as the native Britons. They were
auxiliaries after all, and being in the 4th Cohort meant
they were certainly not the best. On the other hand he

had seen much worse.

He waved his visitor to a stool, the only other seat in his sparsely furnished quarters. Servius Sergius was his optio, his second in command, and from the first moment Caius could see that their relationship was not going to be an easy one.

'So, Servius, you worked with my predecessor. What was he like? And what happened to him?' The optio had narrow saturnine features and looked as if he was permanently sucking a lemon. He did not smile once.

'Your predecessor had been here for some years and was well liked, a just and fair man and fearless in battle. He is sorely missed.' He paused and eyed Caius.

'I suppose you had friends who put you up for this position? I can't imagine why else they would have sent someone all the way from Provincia.' His suppressed anger was obvious and it dawned on the centurion that he had expected to be promoted to his position. Caius doubted anything he could say or do would make the man warm to him and sighed.

'On the contrary, Servius. The truth is they sent me here to get rid of me, not because of any favouritism. But be that as it may I am here now and I expect my orders to be followed to the letter, is that understood? Now tell me about the men.'

The optio stared at him expressionlessly and then launched into a competent and detailed report of the men of the century.

'You still haven't told me what happened to my predecessor,' he said when the man had finished.

'He was killed,' Servius said shortly. 'He was on patrol, there was an ambush, and that was that. Even after all these years this is still a dangerous place. I suggest you remember that.' Caius thanked him and dismissed him. Moments later the girls peeked through the door and came and sat on the floor beside him and for a few minutes he put away the myriad tasks that lay before him.

*

Aurora liked the wall. She was an appealing and attractive girl, and most of the legionaries let her wander the parapet walkways and the more soft-hearted would slip her the odd piece of fruit or occasional sweet bun or biscuit. She was fascinated by the barbarian Britons who approached the wall from time to time to trade, the men in their strange long trousers with hair either in plaits or as wild as that of the women who accompanied them. They would turn up in threes and fours, always careful to approach openly and slowly, holding up the baskets of produce and furs they brought to barter for cloth and sweetmeats and wine and other things difficult or impossible to get north of the wall.

One morning Caius came to their room at the tavern. He was in full armour and marching gear and his centurion's helmet with its impressive plume was tucked under his arm. He told them he was taking his century on a routine patrol on the barbarian side of the wall and might be gone for two or three days.

'Barita and her family are good people and seem to be looking after you well, but I know they can be very busy and I am sure there are times when the tavern is not the most suitable place for young girls. So while I am gone use my room as much as you like. You can both sleep there if you want. Just so you know.' He looked down at them and realised how little time he had been able to spend with them since they arrived. He missed their company sometimes, and yet when they were together he was often at a loss as to what to say.

Aurora in turn looked up and took in the face she knew so well. Close cropped dark hair just starting to go grey at the edges. The nut-brown legacy of Provincia's sun slowly fading from his lined face and determined jaw. Grey eyes that had a permanent faraway look since the death of their mother.

'We'll be fine, *Pater*. Really. Won't we, Aurelia? Don't worry about us.' He smiled and bent down and awkwardly kissed each of them on the cheek. As he straightened up it struck him how tall they had become. They reminded him more and more of their mother, which was simultaneously a joy and a stab to his heart. They were both past their eleventh year and with a shock he realised they were on the threshold of leaving childhood behind them.

'Be good, *carissimae*,' he finally said, and left.

As noon approached the tavern was filling up and the sisters decided to go for a walk. As they wandered aimlessly towards the fort they saw a resplendent group of figures making their way towards them. They recognised Quintus Petronius Urbicus, Prefect of the 4th Gauls and commander of Vindolanda. He was resplendent in a cream silk toga and flanked by his wife and daughter, their hair coiled in the latest style from Rome and wearing flowing pastel robes rich with embroidery.

As they stood back to let them pass the commander's eye fell on the two girls and he stopped and smiled.

'Well, well, what have we here? Where have these two little beauties sprung from? What are your names?'

He was tall and beginning to run to fat. His face which at first glance seemed handsome and winning was marred by greedy eyes and a fleshy, almost pendulous lower lip.

'I am Aurora, sir, and this is my sister Aurelia. We are the daughters of Caius Acilius Verus, the centurion.' He patted their heads and at his touch Aurora shuddered at the unfamiliar and disquieting passions that she felt seething under his bland exterior, unhealthy passions she was too young to fully understand. As it was she just felt somehow soiled and drew back. He threw his head back and laughed.

'You're the shy one, eh? Not like your sister!' Aurora turned and saw that Aurelia had stepped forward and was touching the sleeve of his daughter's robe with an expression of wonder.

'Oh Aurora, it's so soft! And look at the embroidery! How I wish I had a robe like that!' Aurora pulled her away and the threesome walked on, the women shaking their heads and laughing. The commander glanced back over his shoulder and for some reason his speculative expression made Aurora think of a wolf.

While they waited for Caius to return over the next two days Aurelia drove her mad rhapsodizing about the Prefect's women's clothes and jewellery and bemoaning her own simple garments.

*

Caius grimaced as each limping step sent a jolt of

pain through the deep gash in his thigh, securely and competently bandaged though it was. His optio Servius Sergius nodded in sympathy, his saturnine face almost human for once. Their gaze fell on the shuffling group of prisoners in front of them. The ambush had been sudden and unexpected and initially terrifying. The woods seemed to come alive with blue-painted warriors and the air was filled with their war cries. But as so often with the Britons, the attack was reckless, pointless and doomed to failure. As he bellowed commands Caius was pleased to see that his men remembered their training and immediately formed a defensive wall of shields against which the attackers broke like waves on the shore and in minutes most of them were dead and their wounded were despatched soon after.

The Romans lost only two men, their bodies being carried on makeshift stretchers. With a heavy heart Caius followed policy and raided the nearest village, seizing twenty men and women to be sold as slaves and to serve as a warning that this was the consequence of tweaking the Roman tiger's tail.

*

One of the friendlier legionaries told her when the patrol was expected back and Aurora was on the wall soon after dawn, waiting. Aurelia had refused to get up and remained buried under the bedcovers. It was mid-morning when an orderly column two abreast emerged from the tree line in the distance, armour and helmets glinting in the pale sunshine. Soon she could make out Caius' distinctive semi-circle of white and grey plumes, side to side rather than front to back to make him easy for his men to pick out in the heat of battle. Her heart skipped a beat when she saw that he was limping heavily. A gate was opened and the century marched in.

When they were inside the gates closed behind them and Caius bellowed *sta!* and nearly two hundred feet tramped and halted in ragged unison. He shouted *dimito!* and the dismissed men fell out and dispersed. Four legionaries with swords drawn remained to control the huddled group of Britons who were holding on to each other and looking around fearfully. He came over and ruffled her hair.

'So, little one, how have things been? Everything all right? You sister is well? Good.' At that moment the Prefect appeared and surveyed the scene.

'So, centurion - Caius Acilius Verus, isn't it – what happened here?'

Caius gave a succinct report and the prefect nodded.

'Well done, by the book. I like things done by the book. And you are wounded, I see. Do you have a slave, centurion?' Caius shook his head.

'Well, I like to reward men who do well. Pick one of them for yourself before you send them off for auction.'

Aurora had been watching the Britons and her heart went out to them and the uncertain future they faced. Her gaze kept being drawn to one in particular. She looked to be in her thirties and was wrapped in a heavy brown cloak held at the shoulder by an intricately worked and ancient-looking bronze clasp. Her fiery red hair was wild and matted and her startling green eyes were worried but unafraid. Aurora was holding Caius' hand and sensed he was about to refuse. She tugged on it urgently and when he bent down whispered urgently in his ear.

'Pater! The one with the red hair and green eyes! You must ask for her! Please! You must!' Her father looked at the woman and back at his daughter and knew that despite her age she would not have spoken without a reason. He straightened and faced the Prefect, who was watching the scene with raised eyebrows.

'I am most grateful, Prefect. It is an extremely generous gesture. That one, if I may.' He limped over and gestured to the woman, who shrank back. Aurora followed her father and went up to the woman and took her by the hand. The green eyes widened and she nodded imperceptibly and stepped forward.

*

Caius went off to have his wound cleaned and to wash off three days of mud and filth while Aurora led the woman to Caius' room. Aurelia was nowhere to be seen. They sat next to each other on the bed and looked at each other and held each other's hands. To her surprise the woman spoke passable Latin.

'I could not believe it when you touched me,' she said softly. 'Those such as us are rare, so very rare. Do you know what it is, this gift you have?' Aurora shrugged.

'I can see people's thoughts when I touch them. My mother was the same, but my sister isn't and doesn't understand it at all. I think she's jealous.' The woman laughed throatily.

'My name is Vanora, child, and I see you are called Aurora. A pretty name. But I also see you have no idea of what you are capable. Seeing into people's minds is but a small part of what you can do. It does seem to me that we were brought together by the gods. Yours or mine, they are all the same, just with different names. A shame I had to become a slave for it to happen.' She sighed and stroked Aurora's dark locks.

'But I will open your eyes and teach you. I can feel you have great power. Much more than even I. Much more.' Aurelia stood unnoticed in the doorway, watching the strange red-haired woman and her sister holding hands and the familiar feeling of being excluded welled up in her and made her cheeks pink with anger and frustration.

Well I have a secret too, she thought. *You and your silly mind-reading tricks. But I am the one he likes. And I will have pretty things and the other girls will admire me and be envious and so will you Aurora. So will you! Wait and see!*

*

Caius had grown up with slaves and in any case they were ubiquitous in the Empire. But Angerona had always hated the idea of slavery and over the years in the legion he had become used to doing without them. He saw Aurelia in the doorway watching Aurora and the British woman and absently patted her on the head as he went into the room. He sat on the chair and stretched out his leg with a grimace. He had been lucky. An inch to one side and the slashing sword would have severed an artery, but as it was the surgeon's verdict was that the wound was painful but not serious.

Vanora went and knelt before him.

'May I?' she said and before he could respond she had untied the surgeon's bandage and was studying the bloody gash. She put her hand on it and closed her eyes, then motioned to Aurora to kneel next to her.

'Put your hand on the wound, child. Tell me what you sense.'

The first thing Aurora sensed was her father's mixture of irritation and curiosity. She closed her eyes and the other woman's hand covered hers. To her surprise she began to get a sense of the wound's *nature*, and a dawning sense of something dark and unpleasant lurking in the blood and torn tissue. Vanora nodded with satisfaction.

'Very good, Aurora. Astonishing, really, considering you have no training whatsoever. Go and bring me these things.' She listed two common herbs and while Aurora ran to fetch them she busied herself lighting the small brazier that was the room's only heating. Caius studied her quizzically.

'What do you think you are doing, woman?' he said. She looked him in the eye.

'First, my name is Vanora. Second, there is an infection in the wound and if we do not deal with it you may die. So if you know what is good for you let us do what is necessary. You do realise she has great power?' There was a long pause as he digested both the content and the forthright and unafraid delivery of her words. He nodded.

'Yes, I have some idea. I don't know about great, but she has something. Her mother always knew it and meant to nurture it when she was older. But she never had the chance.'

Aurora returned and Vanora instructed her, making her repeat the incantations and then prick her finger and let a drop of blood fall and sizzle in the small fire before making a poultice for the wound and holding her hand over it for several minutes. Caius felt soothing warmth flow from her touch and they helped him to bed and he fell into a deep and dreamless sleep. Nobody noticed Aurelia's absence.

The camp surgeon expressed his surprise at how quickly the wound healed. In the weeks that followed Aurora spent every waking moment with Vanora, learning and absorbing and revelling in every new thing that the older woman showed her as an endless panoply of wonders opened up to her. Caius found himself watching them with quiet enjoyment in his daughter's new-found pleasure.

And, had he been honest with himself, watching the bold, uncompromising red-haired new slave who seemed to have slotted so effortlessly into their lives. Watching the way her body moved under her shapeless shifts and tunics. And in all of this Aurelia was left on the side lines. She professed to be bored and to prefer to be elsewhere and none of them felt the fires of her resentment burning more brightly every day, or thought to ask how she spent her time.

'Why do you stay?' Aurora asked Vanora one day. They were sitting outside watching the moon on a rare crystal clear night.

'You know so much, you could devise a spell to lull the guards and cross the wall any time you wanted, and be free.' She hesitated before finally asking softly, 'Is it just for me?' Vanora thought carefully before answering.

'Yes, it is true I could leave here if I so wished. But now I have met you, and I could not live with myself if I abandoned someone with such rare talents.' She smiled and hugged Aurora.

'You have learned so much, and I still have so

much more to teach you. And I have become … quite fond of you. And your father,' she added as an afterthought. Her face became more serious.

'There is something that we are both guilty of, though. Your sister. Aurelia is deeply troubled, I think. We – you, your father and I – have neglected her of late. We should make an effort to include her more.' Aurora nodded, sombrely.

'You are right, I know that. But it's difficult, isn't it? She can't, you know, do what we do. And she has always been a bit different. She cares about *things*, you see. Pretty clothes and dolls and ornaments and so on. Things that we cannot have because there is no money for them. Even before you came I tried to be closer to her, but we just have so little to say to each other. I loved it when we used to play and laugh together when we were little but as we got older those times became few and far between. And now she avoids my touch because I'll be able to see what is in her mind. But you are right. We should try.'

*

Aurelia's secret place was a corner in an abandoned building outside the vicus that had collapsed years ago. But by squeezing under a fallen beam she had found what was in effect a cave, the entrance hidden by knee-high weeds that grew outside in profusion. She moved a flat stone to one side and pulled her treasures out of a bag. There was enough light filtering through gaps in the fallen roof and masonry for her to see the violet sparkle of the amethyst necklace he had given her. She had never seen let alone possessed anything so beautiful. *A beautiful necklace for a beautiful young woman*, he had said.

She preened remembering it and the way his hand had stroked her cheek. Her smile turned to a fierce frown.

You see, Aurora! He does like me, not you! He gives me gifts, not you and he's the most important man here in Vindolanda! Ha! If you only knew! How jealous you would be!

He had said he had an even better present for her. Pater was away on patrol again and with the century away the barracks were empty. He had told her to wait until everyone was asleep and to slip away from their room at the tavern and to come and meet him in one of the barrack rooms and she quivered with anticipation, trying to imagine what could be even better than the lovely necklace.

*

Aurora and Vanora were at the foot of the stairs leading up to the wall.

'You know what to do. Trust in yourself. You can do this.' Aurora nodded and concentrated. She started murmuring the incantation, making the gestures she had practised, summoning up the force of the god Mannan who had power over mists and fog.

A magic cloud I put on thee, from dog, from cat,
From cow, from horse, from man, from woman,
From young man, from maiden, and from little child.
Till I again return.

The two of them climbed the stairs and walked past the sentry, who half-turned with a puzzled look then shrugged and turned away again. Vanora smiled and when they were some distance away put her lips to Aurora's ear.

'Well done! There are very few who can cast the

spell of invisibility so effectively. I believe you can do almost anything that you set your mind to!'

They turned back and this time the sentry didn't register their passing at all.

*

Aurora and Vanora were fast asleep. Aurelia got off her low bed – more of a pallet, really - very carefully and pulled on her best tunic before tip-toeing out of the room, sandals in hand. Her heart was hammering in her chest as she made her way through the chilly night to the deserted barracks. The door was slightly ajar and she pushed it open and closed it behind her. The only light came from a tiny clay oil lamp. Quintus Petronius Urbicus sat on one of the rough bunk beds and smiled at her, waving her over and patting the bed beside him. She sat down and looked up at him expectantly as he put an arm around her shoulders, enveloping her in a cloud of heavy perfume from his carefully curled and oiled hair.

'So, my little beauty, you came, eh? Wondering what your friend is going to give you tonight?' She nodded, puzzled by the expectant look on his face. Was he expecting her to give him something? But he pulled something from his sleeve and dangled it before her. She gasped and put her hands to her mouth.

It was a beautiful golden chain with intricately worked links from which hung a medallion with the head of a goddess. It glittered like yellow fire in the dim lamplight and Aurelia was entranced. She stretched out a hand but the Prefect held it out of reach.

'I have given you lovely gifts, have I not?' he said. She nodded and he smiled, showing his teeth. 'Well, that's what friends should do, isn't it. Would you like to do something for me?' She nodded again, wondering what she could possibly do for the most powerful man in Vindolanda. There was something in his expression that made her uneasy, a barely suppressed anticipation. He put his hands under her arms and lifted her up.

'Good, good. Come and sit on my lap, there's a good girl, and I will show you.'

*

Servius Sergius shivered and wrapped his cloak tighter around him. His campaign to be useful to the Prefect had led him to be seconded to his staff, and he soon found himself acting as go-between with the girl. And now he was tasked to stand guard and ensure they were not interrupted. *Stupid, vain little creature*, he thought unsympathetically. *So the Prefect likes them young, so what.* Too young for his own tastes, but girls were married off at her age all the time. And it would be one in the eye for that bastard Caius, anyway. Lording it over him in the position that should rightfully have come to him.

His brooding was interrupted by muffled screams from the room followed by a brief commotion and then silence. The door opened and the Prefect beckoned to him.

'Get in here,' he hissed. The optio entered the room and stopped in his tracks. The Prefect's perfectly groomed composure had disappeared and he looked sweaty and dishevelled. The girl lay next to the cooking platform and he saw straight away that she was dead.

'It was her own fault!' said Quintus defensively. 'After all I've done for her the stupid little cow started fighting and screaming. I just hit her to keep her quiet but she fell and hit her head and ... ' he passed a hand over his brow and shook himself. 'What can we do? Nobody must ever know! Ever! Help me and you can have whatever you want!' Servius touched his fingers to the girl's throat but the dent in the side of her head left no doubt that life had fled.

'You've killed her, all right,' he said slowly. 'Now listen to me. That centurion's job should have been mine and I want it now. And gold, a lot of gold. Agree and this will all go away.' The Prefect nodded impatiently.

'Yes, yes, whatever you say. Anything. What do we do now?' The optio looked around and unsheathed his gladiolus.

'First, we bury her. We can't get her past the guards at the gates so it's the only thing to do. Be quick and help me.' They stripped the pathetic little corpse of everything – shoes, clothes, and the cheap trinkets the girl had around her neck and wrist. Servius stuffed them all into a pouch to dispose of later. He went to work with his short sword and worked loose a flagstone in a corner. Together they heaved it up and propped it against the wall and hacked away at the soil. By the time they had excavated a depression a couple of feet deep they were filthy and sweating.

They tried to manhandle the body into it but Aurelia's legs and arms kept sticking out until they tied them together with strips of leather and pushed her down. They covered her with soil and stamped it flat in a macabre dance before carefully replacing the flagstone and filling in the cracks around it.

'I will need some of the gold tomorrow, first thing' he told the Prefect.

'I will have to sweeten the contubernium who live here to close their minds and keep their mouths shut when she begins to smell. At least it's getting colder every day, that will help. Then I suggest we accuse Caius of disposing of his daughter because she rejected his unnatural advances. There will be no proof, but I will think of something and at worst some of the mud will stick. You will dismiss him and appoint me in his place. Are we clear?' The Prefect nodded and regarded the dirt under his fingernails with distaste before he snuffed out the oil lamp and they disappeared into the night.

*

When Caius returned the next morning he was greeted by a sobbing Aurora and a grim-faced Vanora.

'Oh Pater, thank the gods you are back! Aurelia has disappeared! She was there when we went to sleep and she was gone when we woke up! We can't find her anywhere!'

None of them had noticed that Servius Sergius accompanied one of the returning contubernia back to their barrack room, or that the document pouch he often carried seemed unusually heavy.

The three of them were sitting in Caius' room discussing how best to go about searching for her when the door opened and the Prefect entered followed by the optio. Their expressions were grave and Caius got to his feet uncertainly.

'Have you found her?' he asked. They exchanged glances and frowned.

'It's no good pretending, centurion,' Quintus said sternly. We know what you have done. Why not make a clean breast of it and unburden your soul.' Aurora saw her father's jaw drop with an expression of utter bewilderment. She held his hand tightly and felt the force of his confusion.

'We know you were having unnatural relations with her, so don't attempt to deny it. You crept into the camp last night and disposed of her, hoping nobody would suspect because you were camped beyond the wall. But we have eight witnesses who saw you creeping away from the camp in the dead of night.'

Aurora felt fury and outrage building in her father like a volcano about to erupt and she felt the same thing happening inside her. She threw herself at the Prefect and optio who caught her by an arm each. The commander laughed nastily.

'Oh, was this one jealous then? I suppose you were having both … ' but Aurora tore herself free and stumbled backwards into Vanora's arms. Her eyes were wide with shock and horror and she pointed a trembling hand at the commander.

'Pater! Pater! It was him! He killed her and … ' the optio and Caius drew their swords with a synchronised whisper of steel on leather. Servius whistled and the men of the contubernium next door began to crowd in through the narrow door, swords drawn. He had been generous with his gold and they were his now.

Caius looked at his daughter and was about to ask her if she was sure but her awful expression gave him his answer.

'Seize him!' barked the Prefect. The soldiers started forward and Caius held his sword in front of him, daring one of them to be the first. They had all seen him in battle and were none too keen to be the first to approach the unwavering gladiolus and his murderous glare, suffused with terrible pain and fury. They froze into a tableau when Aurora opened her mouth.

Something in her had snapped. In her brief contact she had seen the vile way the Prefect had dealt with her sister and caught a glimpse of the optio's desperate wish for advancement and how he had helped to hide the body. She had even seen him fleetingly remember how he had disposed of the previous centurion but that was something she would only remember later. Right now all she had in her mind was that they had murdered Aurelia and unceremoniously put her body under the floor like so much garbage and then dared to make vile accusations against her father.

It was as if some force had taken her over and she knew exactly what to do. In an instant she whipped out her little knife and cut her arm, smearing the blood over her hands and launching into the incantation that summoned Elphane, invoking the goddess in her aspects of death and destruction.

They all watched her, frozen in disbelief. She seemed to grow taller and her body thrummed with energy. Her voice sounded older and rang with authority as ancient words flowed from her and her bloody hands stretched commandingly and accusingly at the men before her.

They started to look confused and then terrified

and then one of the soldiers screamed and hacked at the optio, severing his arm in a fountain of blood. Now they were all screaming like madmen and stabbing and slashing at each other. Caius and Vanora backed away until their backs were against the wall as the carnage unfolded. Gouts of bright red blood splashed everywhere and men were falling like ninepins and in what seemed like no time at all the last two simultaneously thrust into each other's throats and sank gurgling to the floor still gripping the swords they had fatally embedded in each other.

Aurora slumped to the floor, drained. Caius and Vanora picked her up and put her on the bed.

'What did you do, child. Gods, what did you do?' Her eyes fluttered open and her smile was pitiless and without humour.

'I made them all think the others were huge ravening bears with long fangs and claws like scythes and they did the rest themselves,' she said. 'Oh. Pater, poor Aurelia. She didn't deserve this.' Vanora stroked her brow and made her sit up.

'Do you remember the spell you used on the wall? On the guards? We must leave now, this very minute. We can never explain this and nobody will ever believe us. Aurora! Now! It must be now!'

They could hear a commotion outside, a hubbub of uncertain voices asking each other what had caused all the screaming. Aurora nodded and took both their hands.

'They will not be able to see us, Caius,' said Vanora. 'Hold our hands and follow us and keep silent. Trust in your daughter.'

Aurora took a deep shuddering breath and began the incantation.

A magic cloud I put on thee ...

They stepped through the door only feet away from a group of approaching soldiers and had to hurry to get out of their way. The first one to enter the room was a young and inexperienced legionary who stumbled back outside a moment later and vomited copiously onto the paving. Vanora looked back and saw their bloody footprints following them like an accusing snake but then they stepped onto grass and the trail stopped. The gate was opening to let in a wagon filled with hay for the horses and they slipped out and walked away from Vindolanda forever.

*

Caius and Vanora stood before an ancient stone altar in the midst of a grove of venerable oaks that let in so little light it was as if they were submerged in a dark green sea. They had flowers in their hair and Aurora blessed them with one incantation after another to ensure happiness, to ward off evil, and to live long and fruitful lives.

Through indirect contacts amongst the Britons in the vicus Vanora had heard that the whole affair had been hushed up and the official report described an ambush in which the ten men had died fighting heroically against impossible odds.

Other soldiers superstitiously refused to use either Caius' or the room that had belonged to the doomed contuburnium and they were eventually used as storerooms.

And every year a shadow seemed to flit across the wall and a mass of wildflowers mysteriously appeared in front of the doorway.

A note on Vindolanda from the author

I have tried to stay within the confines of what is known and what is current theory based on scientific, archaeological and forensic fact. There seems little doubt that a child aged between 9 and 11 was murdered and hastily hidden under the flagstones in a barrack room at the Roman fort of Vindolanda by Hadrian's Wall, and that it occurred somewhere between 213 and 230 AD. Most unusually, no artefacts of any kind were found with the body – no buttons, shoe studs, adornments, cloth or leather fragments – absolutely nothing.

Forensic analysis of the remains suggest the arms were bound at the elbows, that there was trauma to the head, that the child had not performed hard manual work, was healthy, and not suffering from malnutrition. Isotope analysis of surviving tooth enamel indicates the child was almost certainly not a local but came from an area broadly covering Spain, Southern France or Italy, and had been at Vindolanda for less than three to four years. The bone sizes indicate a height of about 4' 7" or 1.5 metres.

It seems certain that the 4th Cohort of Gauls were the garrison at Vindolanda at this time and their prefect and commander at some point between 222 and 235 AD was a Quintus Petronius Urbicus, who set up an altar to Jupiter that also tells us his family came from Brescia in Italy. The Roman army structure of eight-man contubernium, ten contubernium century with its centurion, and six century cohort as well as the tightly-knit nature of these eight-man units are also based on current historical understanding, as are the weapons, armour and clothing.

There are several accounts of the body found at Vindolanda on the web, one of which is below.

http://www.thehistoryblog.com/archives/19387

Nighthawks

Cities, like cats, will reveal themselves at night.

Rupert Brooke

Edward Hopper painted Nighthawks in 1942. As with so many of his paintings it is a disturbing study in urban alienation and when I looked at it again recently I started wondering about the people in the picture. What were their stories?

It was late. The kind of late that makes you wonder if you're maybe the only one left after some disaster that happened when you weren't looking. An alone kind of late. Late on the kind of night that holds its breath and wraps loneliness around you like a shroud.

I had just finished a case and had a roll of bills in my pocket and it felt good. Each dollar was another brick in the wall that shut me off from the rest of the world. The client was fat and balding and thought his wife was playing around with his buddy. I followed her for a week and she wasn't. He didn't believe me and didn't want to pay. He hit my fist with his chin and changed his mind.

It wasn't my part of town and my stomach was telling me it was time to put something in it. I saw a diner on a street corner. The place had plate glass walls wrapped around both sides like a big goldfish bowl and washed the grey sidewalk with white neon. It said *Phillies* and I wondered what had happened to the apostrophe. Maybe it got a better job and left. But it looked clean and I was hungry and I went in and sat at the counter. It was made of heavy varnished mahogany and the guy behind it looked like he was in the trenches waiting to be attacked.

He had the kind of young / old face that kept you guessing and changing your mind every time the light hit it from another angle. He wore an impressively clean white jacket with *Joe* machine embroidered in red satin thread over his heart and a jaunty white soda-jerk cap. His hair was yellow and cropped so short I wondered why he hadn't gone all the way and had his head shaved. He stopped wiping the counter and smiled. His teeth were like a crooked picket fence and told me I should be guessing old not young.

'Evenin', Mister,' he said, 'what'll it be?' I settled my haunches on a padded vinyl barstool and looked up and down the counter. There were little groups of paper napkins and sugar and salt and ketchup and nothing else.

'I'm in the mood for a menu,' I said and it took him a second before he laughed, a high-pitched whinnying kind of noise. He might or might not be a nice guy, but that laugh told me he probably didn't have a wife or a girlfriend. Or maybe he got lucky and found a nice deaf girl. He dug out a laminated menu card from under the counter and slid it towards me like he didn't want to get too close in case I bit him. It had *Phillies* in fancy letters at the top and the apostrophe was still AWOL. I scanned it and my guts rumbled.

'Hungry, huh,' he said. As a conversational gambit it wasn't up there with the greatest but I could see he was trying to be friendly so I stopped myself saying, *No I always go into diners and look at the menu when I'm really full.* I flipped the menu back onto the counter.

'Coffee, black, and a burger, rare,' I said. He nodded and disappeared through a yellow door for about five seconds before returning. I could see his wheels turning as he tried to come up with something else to say. It was kinda sad to watch so I just sat and waited. Then the door opened and two people came in and he was off the hook. They sat down on the other side of the counter, not next to me, but not opposite either.

Under the shadow of his fedora the man's eyes were like dead black chips of ice. His thin angular face was grey and looked like it had promised never to smile and was sticking to it. His suit was expensive and his tie was silk. Now I'm not a guy who radiates goodwill and joy to all mankind. I'm a guy who makes people look away real quick if they make the mistake of catching my eye. But this guy was something else. He was like a walking corpse and radiated coldness I could feel ten feet way.

The woman had seen better days but I guessed she had once been a looker and she still filled out her red dress in all the right places. Her hair was red too, the kind of red that comes out of a bottle. Her life was etched in fine lines around her eyes and mouth. I knew the look and I knew she was carrying some kind of baggage. On the other hand who wasn't? She looked nervous and like she was gonna faint and avoided looking at Dead Eyes.

He saw me watching them and stared at me. I guess he was as used to people looking away as I was but I held his gaze and kept my face expressionless and then the redhead said something and he turned away. But not before a last look that said, *this ain't over.*

They ordered coffee and sat not looking at each other and not talking and I wondered why they were together. Joe put down a mug of coffee in front of me and then two more in front of them. Silence hung in the air like a gunshot about to happen and Joe started humming under his breath. I knew something wasn't right and he could feel it too. He pushed the sugar dispenser towards the couple and the man's hand clamped on Joe's arm like a striking cobra.

'Can the symphony,' he said. 'I don't like it.' His voice was like chalk on a blackboard and without any sort of emotion. Joe stopped humming and nodded with his eyes wide and the man let him pull his arm away and he scuttled to the far end of the counter as far away from Dead Eyes as he could get.

The yellow door banged open and the redhead jumped, her hand to her mouth. The guy didn't react at all. A Latino in a T-shirt that had once been white back when dinosaurs roamed the earth banged down my burger on the counter and disappeared again trailing invisible streamers of sweat and grease behind him. Joe picked up my burger and put it in front of me with a knife and fork and a plastic squeeze bottle of ketchup that had aged gracefully to a colour somewhere between grey and curdled cream.

I picked up the burger and took a bite and it was good, really good. My stomach sighed in relief as the first consignment of salt, protein and fat headed south. Dead Eyes stood up and made a big show of sniffing the air and wrinkling his nose.

'Something in here stinks,' he announced to nobody in particular. I ignored him and took another mouthful. He looked mildly surprised at the lack of reaction so he tried again.

'Like I said, something in here stinks.' He looked straight at me. 'Maybe it's that shitburger or maybe it's the piece of shit eating it.' I could feel meat juice running down my chin. I put down the burger and wiped it off with a paper napkin. I ignored him and took a swig of hot coffee. I could see he was getting really steamed because I wasn't reacting the way I was supposed to.

'Deaf as well, huh. Maybe you can't taste anything either and that's how come you can shovel shit like that into your mouth.' He paused and just in case I still hadn't got the message he added, 'I'm talking to you, shitface.'

He obviously liked the word and I couldn't blame him. It's a good solid all-purpose word that lets off steam. I've been known to use it myself. I'd ignored him up to then but now I sighed and put the coffee back on the counter and looked him straight in the eye. I knew guys like him. No soul and nothing but hate and the desperate need to be feared. That was all they knew. I spoke slowly as if I was explaining something to a not very bright kid.

'I'm sitting here minding my own business. So were you and Red over there. So now if you and your pea-brain are set on making this something else why don't you come over here and tell me about it. It's not far, even you should be able to find your way. Maybe two steps straight ahead, turn left. Think you can manage that?'

His face had gone a sickly red and it wasn't much of an improvement on the grey. He made an inarticulate noise and grinned like a skull and as he moved towards me a switchblade appeared in his hand like a conjuring trick and flicked open and I threw the mug of coffee in his face.

He screamed and the blade clattered on the floor as he clutched his eyes. I sighed and got up. I really didn't want to do this but if I didn't I knew he would kill me. So I let him have it with a right hook to the belly and as he folded over I grabbed his hair and pulled his head down and brought up my knee and his nose crunched. Maybe some teeth as well. I didn't know and I didn't care. He was writhing on the floor and I kicked him between the legs and his hands kept fluttering to and fro as he kept changing his mind about whether he should cradle his face or his crotch.

There was a nasty stain on the knee of my pants. I blotted the worst of it with a paper napkin and reached down and plucked a wallet from his hip pocket. I pulled out a ten and stuffed it into my pocket and threw another on the counter.

'One bill's for the dry cleaner and the other's for the shitburger. No hard feelings.' I dropped the wallet on the floor and headed for the door. The redhead grabbed my arm as I passed by her.

'You shouldn't have done that, Mister, He's mean, real mean. He's gonna come after you now.' I shrugged but she wouldn't let go. She looked at me and down at Dead Eyes who was still fully preoccupied with his personal universe of pain. I could see she was having some kind of inner struggle as emotions chased each other across her face like frightened ghosts. She held onto my arm and got to her feet.

'Take me with you, Mister. I … just please take me with you. I can't be here when he gets up.' There was desperation in her voice and I've always been a sucker for a damsel in distress. It's gotten me into a lot of trouble over the years but I guess learning from my mistakes has never been my strong point. I wasn't even sure I had any strong points. I nodded and we left the diner and stood on the pavement. I saw Joe picking up a phone and guessed he wanted the cops around when Dark Eyes started looking for somebody to blame. That's what guys like him always do.

'Where do you wanna go?' I asked. She was hanging onto my arm so tightly I was losing the feeling in my fingers.

'You've got a place, dontcha?' she said. I nodded.

There were no cabs around that time of night. There was nothing much of anything around. We walked to the subway and took the train back into my part of town. Another walk and I let us into the dingy brownstone where I live and work. Two flights up and she stopped in front of my door. It had *Matt Stone, Private Investigator* inscribed on it in peeling gold script and she turned and looked at me wide-eyed. Under the dim low-watt hall light you couldn't see the lines and her eyes were the green of summer lawns and her red dress clung to her figure in a way that reminded me of Zelda. Thinking about Zelda still hurt so I pushed away the memories and nodded and let us in, locking the door behind me.

'You're a private eye!' she said as if it was something special. I stopped myself explaining to her that it wasn't. I showed her where the bedroom was and picked up a spare blanket and told her I'd sleep on the sofa in my office. She held my arm and turned me around and kissed me. I wasn't expecting it and it felt real good and went on for longer than either of us intended.

'Thank you,' she said softly. 'Thank you for getting me away from him and for letting me stay here.' I nodded and headed for the office. I took a bottle of bourbon out of a filing cabinet and poured a slug into a glass. The glass wasn't clean but I figured what the hell, alcohol would kill anything that might have taken up residence. I knocked it back and fiery warmth spread down my chest and that felt good too. I had another and hit the sagging leather couch.

I dreamed I was in the diner and no matter what I did Dead Eyes kept bouncing off the floor and asking for a coffee and a shitburger and each time I knocked him down he bounced right up again. Then the dream switched and I was in my bed and a redhead was alternating between kissing me and shaking me. I came awake and realised the shaking part was real and the kissing was in the dream. Life's like that.

She was sitting on the edge of the couch wearing a threadbare old silk robe of mine. I tried to remember where I had got it and couldn't. I could feel the heat of her thigh pressed against mine and when she saw I was awake she stopped shaking my shoulder.

I sat up and lit up a Camel and gave her one too. Night was on the way out and the dirty grey light filtering through the window mirrored the city streets below.

'I'm sorry I woke you up', she said, 'but there are things I gotta tell you and I couldn't sleep any more and I thought I was gonna go nuts if I didn't tell somebody.'

She took a deep drag and blew out a big plume of smoke that hung in the air like an unanswered question as she tried to find the words. My night was shot anyway so I let her take her time. Finally she turned and looked me in the eyes.

'I'm Gabby, Gabby Green.' She smiled and her face transformed and I became aware of her thigh against mine again.

'My friends call me Gee-Gee,' she went on and stuck out her hand. 'Hello, Matt Stone, Private Investigator.' She took another deep drag and went on.

'I was a secretary in a lawyer's office, a guy called Ed Rossi. He didn't seem to have a lot of clients but was always dressed real sharp, one of those guys who only want the best, you know? He was fine with me, didn't try anything funny like other creeps I've worked for. Always friendly. There wasn't that much work and as often as not he'd tell me to go early or take the afternoon off, like that. It was real nice, the best job I've ever had.' She paused and dropped her cigarette into a mug of three day old coffee I'd left on the floor. It hissed like a drowning snake. I did the same.

'Then about a month ago it started to change. He was still fine with me but you could see he was worried about something. He was out a lot, meeting with clients, he said. Then one day I hear him unlocking the big safe he has in his office and he comes out to me carrying a bag. Kind of like a big leather briefcase, you know? And he asks me to keep it in my rooms – I'd just rented a little place in the Village.'

'Hide it, Gabby, he says, 'hide it good and don't tell nobody about it. Anybody asks you don't know nothin', got it?'

She started trembling and leaned against me. It seemed natural to put my arm around her. She was soft and smelled like a woman should, sweet and warm and musky. Her robe slipped and I tried not to stare at the swell of her ample breasts. Silk slides real easy and every time she moved against me it slid down a little more. I tried to focus on what she was saying but it was hard.

Her face was inches from mine and her lips were soft and red and I don't know exactly how it happened but we were kissing and the silk robe gave up and slid sulkily to the floor. Her skin was like alabaster and my hands were leading a life of their own and my clothes decided to keep the robe company on the floor. It had been a long time since Zelda but I let Gee-Gee's urgent movements push away my memories and let myself sink into the moment and it felt good. Very good.

Afterwards we lit another couple of Camels and I draped the robe over us and Gee-Gee started talking again.

'Like I was saying, Ed gave me this bag to keep for him. Then this morning I get a message from my landlady and she says Ed called and says to take the day off. Well, that was fine by me but then I remembered there was a letter on my desk I was meant to post. It was kind of important, some legal document, and I didn't have any plans so I thought I'd just drop in and take care of it and maybe do some shopping afterwards.' She shuddered.

'I went in and there was this guy there – the one you knocked around in the diner. He told me Ed was busy and I should leave. I knew something was wrong and asked him who he was. He said his name was Jimmy Di Leto and – Jeez, you saw how creepy he was. I was getting scared and headed for the door. Suddenly he's grabbing my arm.'

'You're the secretary, right? he says. Maybe you know where he kept it, yeah, I bet you do know. What about it, doll?'

'The door to Ed's office was pushed open just a crack and I could see the sole of a shoe through the crack. Not moving. I looked into the creep's eyes and it was like I was a bug and he'd step on me without thinking twice. They were just empty and I was getting more scared every minute. So when he kept asking and asking I told him what Ed had given me. He just nodded and said, that's better, that's being a smart broad, and I knew, I just knew he was going to kill me as soon as he had the bag. He took me downstairs and the diner's just around the corner. I was shaking and my legs started giving out and I said, I'm too shaky to walk, take me to the diner, just let me have a coffee and I'll be okay. Please. He shrugged and said okay, one coffee, why not, and that's how we ended up there.'

'Did you give him your address?' I asked. She shook her head and the robe slipped off us and I ran my hands down her curves and sighed. I was doing that a lot lately. Maybe I'd caught some sighing disease. But my brain was working again and I reluctantly pushed her away and sat up.

'Honey, we gotta get that bag before Jimmy gets his act together. Dammit. We shoulda gone last night. C'mon, we gotta move.' Ten minutes later we were in a cab. She started to give the address but I stopped her and made him take us to Grand Central. I like Grand Central. I don't go to churches because I figure if there is a God He's been otherwise occupied for some time now. But this place is a cathedral in honour of people, and good or bad – mostly bad – I know about people. We walked through the station and out the other side and took another cab and I told her to get the cabbie to drop us a few minutes away from her place.

It was a brownstone not unlike mine and she let us in. She led the way to the top floor and I was breathing heavy by the time we got there. Maybe I was out of shape. Or maybe it was watching the roll of her nicely rounded rear all the way up. The place was nice, mostly old stuff but good and solid. She went to the bed and got on her knees and dragged out an expensive-looking leather briefcase and put it on the bed.

'Do you know what's in it?' I asked. She shook her head. It had a fancy brass lock that wouldn't open so I pulled out my pocket knife and a minute later it was dangling from a strip of leather and the briefcase wasn't expensive any more. I opened it and it was stuffed with bills, tens and hundreds. There were a lot of them. She gasped and closed it again.

'C'mon, we need to get outta here,' I said and picked it up and she followed me to the door. I opened it and stared down the barrel of a .357 Magnum. I recognised it because I had one like it in a holster clipped to my waistband in the small of my back. I hate carrying a gun but the only thing I hate even more is not having one when I need it. Looking at it from this end the hole was a dark tunnel to hell. Behind it was Dead Eyes. Or Jimmy Di Leto as I now knew he was called.

Somehow knowing his name wasn't much of a comfort and I saw murder in his black eyes glittering on either side of a gleaming white bandage taped over his nose. He made shooing motions with the barrel and Gee-Gee gasped as I backed into the room with the end of the barrel a couple of inches from my face.

When you're holding a gun on someone it's not a great idea to be real close to them. It kind of takes away a lot of the advantage but he was too full of rage and the triumphant desire to crow and make me beg to think straight. I glanced over his shoulder and let myself smile and being human he turned to see who was behind him. Being human is a bitch. My fist mashed the bandage into his face and he screamed and I knocked the gun out of his hand and he fell back. Then there was a jolt of white hot pain and everything went dark.

Somebody was playing bongo drums on the back of my head and the ripples of pain made me groan. I opened my eyes and looked up and Gee-Gee was standing over me. She was holding the Magnum, which was good because it meant Dead Eyes wasn't a threat any more. She was pointing it at me and I couldn't figure out why and that was bad.

I levered myself up to a sitting position and she stepped back. The gun never wavered and I was getting a very bad feeling.

'What's going on, Gee-Gee? What happened?' My voice was rough as three day stubble and she smiled. There was no warmth in it and I started feeling cold. I turned my head and saw Dead Eyes lying on his back a couple of feet away. His face was turned towards me and he had a third eye in the middle of his forehead and lay in a spreading halo of dark blood.

'Not much of a private eye, are you,' she said. I don't know what it is with bad guys. And bad dolls. When they have the drop on you they have this need to gloat, to tell you how smart they are. It's saved me more than once.

'I'm beginning to get the picture,' I said, 'So who is the stiff really? Was any of it true?' She nodded like I was a slow schoolboy who was finally getting it.

'I guess I don't mind telling you.' She sat on the edge of the bed and crossed her legs. Even in this situation I couldn't help admiring them as the nylon caught the light and highlighted their smooth curves.

'His name *is* Jimmy Di Leto, but what I didn't tell you was that he was Ed's partner. Rossi & Di Leto, they called themselves. They were bent and their clients were mostly crooks and they didn't just help them with legal stuff. They helped them turn dirty money into nice Persil whiter than white money. I wasn't supposed to know but if you're nosy like me you pick up on things.' She was starting to look bored as if telling me how smart she had been wasn't turning out to be as satisfying as she had thought. That wasn't good. But she continued and I started breathing again.

'So I overheard them saying one of their clients was bringing in a lot of cash for them to work their magic on.' She nudged the mutilated briefcase with her foot.

'A hundred thousand bucks. I used to snoop around their desks when they were out and knew that Ed kept the safe combination taped under a drawer. So after this guy went into Ed's office with a big bag and came out without it I knew it was time to make my move.' She sighed and frowned.

'It shoulda been easy. Jimmy was supposed to be out of town for the day and Ed was in court. I opened the safe and there it was. Ever seen a hundred thousand dollars before, Matt? I hadn't. And when I stuffed it into Ed's briefcase all I could see was a new life, a good life. But then Ed walked in and I had to shoot him. Yeah, that's right, the gun's mine.'

'I don't mind telling you it shook me up. I'd never killed anybody before and I felt kinda bad - Ed had been okay to me, you know? Anyways I took the cash back here and then I realised all the paperwork on me was still in the office. If I could get rid of that then nobody, not even Jimmy, would know where to find me. He never had anything to do with that side of things – it was only ever Ed who paid me and knew where I lived.'

'So I go back and clean out the files and then Jimmy walks in. He saw Ed's body and had that damn knife of his at my throat before I knew what was happening. He took the gun out of my purse and the rest is pretty much what I told you before.'

She was at the end of her story and there was only one loose end. Me. I started to sweat. I took one hand off the floor and felt around the back of my head and winced. I had a bump so big it was gonna look like I had two heads. My other hand was propping me up and it was behind me where she couldn't see it and I slowly manoeuvred it to my back.

She saw me wince and grinned.

'Sorry about that – I guess it must hurt a lot, huh.' Her grin faded and I could see I had run out of time. Her gun came up and pointed at me. Her hand was steady.

'I'm sorry, Matt. Really. You tried to help me and you seem like an okay kinda guy. But I can't take no chances.' I pointed to the bag with the cash.

'What about that?' I said and she was human too and glanced down and that was all I needed. My Magnum was already in my hand and I brought it around and her mouth started to open and the sound of the shot was deafening and a little red hole appeared in the centre of her forehead. Blood and brains spattered on the faded wallpaper behind her like a too-bright Jackson Pollock and she fell to the floor.

I got up and stood over them. Dead Eyes and Gee-Gee's third eyes were staring at each other as if puzzled. Like they were asking, *how did we get here?*

'Greed,' I said and holstered my piece. I picked up

the briefcase and looked out of the door. The corridor was deserted and I climbed out of the window onto the fire escape. Minutes later I was just another anonymous schmuck in the crowds on the sidewalk.

ABOUT THE AUTHOR

Michael Anderson was born in Bombay (now Mumbai) in India where he grew up and went to school, travelling widely in Europe on occasional extended visits. He left India at the age of 18 and after a year at the University of Göttingen in Germany settled in London, where he has lived ever since.

He has a degree in Medieval History from the University of London and has had a variety of jobs including Bollywood movie extra, fork lift truck driver, and freelance accountant. His passions are writing, history, and music, and he has several writing projects currently underway.

Apart from writing, he occasionally composes classical music and plays jazz bass when the opportunity arises.

This is his second collection of short stories. The first, Gardening By Moonlight, appeared as an e-book in 2011 and as a paperback in 2013.

Visit Michael's website at

www.michaelanderson.org